I0772956

KEEPING SUSANNA SAFE

By

Florence Witkop

ISBN-13: 978-1-965352-04-5

I had a place to go. A summer rental. I'd made a deposit and signed a lease. So with the key in my purse, I did what I'd been planning to do since being passed over for promotions so many times I'd gotten sick of being invisible.

I quit.

My bosses weren't happy.

"Are you sure this is what you want?" There was an undercurrent in the room as they read and then re-read my resignation. They'd not paid any attention to me while I was employed so why the exit interview?

I'd answered politely. "Yes I'm sure it's what I want."

The unreadable faces of the men across the table let the silence drag on forever until finally one of them asked, "Why are you quitting?"

Again I answered politely. "Because I wish to pursue other opportunities."

They looked at one another and then back at me

and something about their expressions sent a shiver through me as one of them, it didn't matter which because they were clones of each other, spoke in a voice that was meant to be placating and wasn't. "You'll stick by the non-disclosure agreement you signed when you were hired."

I was a lowly clerk. The possibility of my knowing company secrets was so ridiculous I almost laughed. And they made toys. No secrets there. "Of course I will."

But they continued to stare at me and mentally take me apart until I got so tired of playing nice that I added to my answer in the most scathing tone of voice I could manage. "Besides, the NDA is only important if you break the law."

I was so tired of their superior attitude that I spit out my next words. "And you don't do that, do you? You don't break the law. Do you?" Then I stared at them and folded my arms across my chest as I dared them to respond.

They continued to look at me with no expression at all until one of them said, "Of course we don't."

And just like that I was dismissed and minutes later my desk was empty and I held my head high as I headed for the elevator and left their office forever.

Good riddance!

Two days later I was hundreds of miles away in the lovely place promised by the ad that had caught my attention. The cottage in the picture was rustic and pretty and the ad had promised peace and a tree dotted rural countryside but the price had been beyond my means until it was lowered because no one was interested.

Then it was lowered again. And then again and again until it was in my price range. I'd answered the ad but offered half what it asked because I'm a canny negotiator. Eventually, probably because no one else wanted to spend the summer there, my final, low-ball offer was accepted.

Now I was here with a murmuring creek mere yards from my rented cottage. It was perfect. Quiet and peaceful yet with the high-speed internet access that was important to my future and somewhat unusual so far from a large city.

It was a totally rural environment with gravel roads instead of paved ones and a handful of houses scattered about in no particular order near the few stores that made up what must be the town itself.

My immediate thought as I closed the car door and looked around was that the nearby creek was calling to me so instead of checking out my new home I went towards the sound.

The ground was soft from the recent winter thaw with spots of dirty snow still remaining in shady places and as I walked towards that murmuring creek my high heels sank in deeply enough that I removed them and walked in my stocking feet. Then I tugged my stockings off, too, and let my toes wriggle in the cold mud as the sound of rushing water became a lovely background to the arguments of a million birds hiding in the huge, old shade trees just showing the first hint of spring green.

As I drew closer to that murmuring creek I smiled complacently. Yep, I'd done the right thing to drop out of civilization in order to take a few-- or many -- on-line courses to upskill my resume, chat up a few people I'd met online who could connect me with better jobs than the one I'd just left, and generally redirect and restart my career in any city big enough to hold the kind of company that would see my value and never pass me up for promotion. Ever.

I studied the soggy ground ahead of me. The winter thaw wasn't complete but the sun had warmed the exposed soil enough that it wasn't too cold on my bare feet and the squishy mud felt good as I walked far enough to see the creek itself.

Then I stopped breathing because what I saw was so perfect that for a moment I didn't believe it was real.

That *he* was real.

That the tall, dark haired and very, very well-built man in the middle of the creek whipping a line back and forth in the time-tested motion guaranteed to cause the brightly colored, artificial lure on the end of his fly-fishing line to drop precisely in the center of a small, quiet eddy that surely held a trout or two wasn't a figment of my imagination. Or whatever kind of fish swam in the crystal clear water.

He didn't know I was there and I didn't make my presence known. Instead I simply enjoyed the sight. He was poetry in motion. Real life art. The wind ruffled his hair and the surface of the water equally, the sun shone on both man and creek and the budding branches above moved slightly and turned both creek and man into a dance of water and light.

Then a fish struck his line and he played it slowly, patiently, muscles working as he let the line out and then back until he added what looked like a trout to the creel at his waist. I clapped. Startled, he turned towards me.

My breath stopped because he was the guy I'd created in my imagination one piece at a time starting when I was a little girl. Tall, dark hair, with eyes I couldn't make out at that distance, muscles everywhere but not overdone. An outdoor guy, I decided, which description jibed with the fishing gear and the experienced way he'd put his lure exactly where he wanted.

We stood there like two idiots and simply stared at one another. I stepped closer, holding my high heels in one hand, intending to introduce myself as his head tipped a bit in surprise because he clearly didn't recognize me and, as I thought about it, I realized that in such a small place everyone knew everyone else so my appearance must be a shock not to mention that I was still wearing clothes more suited to the city than a small town.

I wanted to explain. To get to know someone in my new home. To be friendly because that was probably the way things were done here and to find out if he was real or a figment of my imagination.

I took another step so he could hear me over the sound of the creek. I stepped to the bank of the creek overlooking the rushing water and then still another step onto the ground that was overhanging the creek. It seemed solid.

It wasn't.

The ground gave way beneath me and I found myself falling into that sparkling, clean water. I screamed, a knee-jerk reaction to falling as I dropped into water that was only a few feet deep but was ice cold, probably only recently thawed. I would have screamed again but the cold stole my breath.

Before I could get my bearings, a hand grabbed my arm and pulled me upright. My hero was inches from me, fly rod in one hand and me in the other, inspecting my wet body. Then I started to shiver.

"You're cold," he said unnecessarily. I wrapped my arms around myself but it did little good. I felt like I'd been dumped naked into a snowbank in the middle of winter. "We need to get you warm." He looked around. "Let's get you into the sunshine. That'll help. And I believe you need my shirt more than I do."

He steered me out of the creek with his one free hand and headed us both towards the sunshine that surrounded my new rental cottage. As soon as we left the shade of the trees that arched over the creek and kept the last vestiges of winter snow intact in small, protected spots I felt warmer. Somewhat.

"Thanks." I was so cold I could barely speak as I shivered uncontrollably. He divested himself of the creel around his waist and started to remove his shirt. "Not necessary," I managed as I shivered harder but was still marginally able to talk.

I pointed to the cottage. "It's mine, at least for the summer." I had to stop speaking momentarily as a severe wave of shivering swept through me but it subsided enough that I could speak once more. "At least it will be when I go inside." I pointed to my car. "I have all kinds of clothes." I looked at him. "I'll be fine."

Another shiver, worse than the last, stopped my speech for a moment. "And thanks."

Then as the sun did its work and I knew I'd survive I added before another bout of shivering caught hold of me. "You were awesome back there."

His face lit up as his eyes still swept my soaking self from top to bottom and back again. "You fly fish?"

"I used to. A million years ago with my grandfather. Not since then, though." No place to fish in the city.

The shivering returned and this time it was more violent and lasted longer. He stopped sizing me up and said, "I'll help carry your stuff in. You can shower to get warm while I bring in your bags."

I should have said I could do it myself. I'm totally capable of carrying a few suitcases. But I didn't. Instead, I said, "Thanks," and headed for the door of my rental cottage with my arms still wrapped around my sopping, frozen body.

I started to insert the key but stopped at his chuckle. "It's not locked." I turned to him in surprise. "No place here is locked." He shrugged and well-developed muscles moved in his shoulders. "No reason to lock anything in Southfork."

I pushed the door open and stepped inside and hoped I'd not drip enough that I'd have to mop the floor because I didn't know if a mop or even a broom came with the place. I decided I could use a towel. I'd brought several of those.

He'd already grabbed two suitcases and followed me inside. "So Mrs. Sanders actually rented this place." His voice said he was surprised.

"I watched the ad for weeks. When the rent

dropped to my budget I called and offered even less." Said between shivers.

"And she took it and was happy to have someone here for the summer," he said, still chuckling as he looked around for a place to put the suitcases. "She checked out other ads to know what to charge. We told her this isn't the city and that small town, seasonal cottages rent for less. But we couldn't convince her. She thinks people should pay more for places as lovely as Southfork."

"It is beautiful." I wrapped my arms around my shivering body as he deposited my suitcases in the middle of the floor and another bout of shivering overcame me that was the worst yet.

"You should take a hot shower and you should take it now." He pointed to a door. "That's the bathroom. I'll bring in the rest of your things while you thaw."

I grabbed the smaller of the suitcases because it held whatever I'd needed during my trip including a couple changes of clothes and headed for the bathroom and water as hot as I could get it. It wasn't too long before I was luxuriating in a steamy, hot, hot, hot shower.

When I reluctantly got out because if I stayed too long I'd use up all the hot water and get cold all over again I spent an inordinate amount of time toweling myself and getting the knots out of my hair while wondering for the millionth time why I left it long because I went through this same agony whenever it got tangled which was pretty much daily as I wished, also for the millionth time, that I was larger than I am and more in shape because if I was I might not have needed rescuing.

Chapter 2

I exited the bathroom expecting to see all my luggage in the middle of the floor and my savior gone. Instead I saw his back as he stood at the kitchen sink cleaning what looked like a fair amount of fish on a counter covered with old newspapers while whistling a tuneless song.

I stared at him silently because even up close he hadn't lost the appeal I'd felt earlier. If anything it had gone up a notch. He was the kind of guy I'd always wanted to meet and never had. My lower self turned warm just watching those economical, practiced movements.

When he realized I was done with my shower, he turned and my insides grew even warmer and fuzzy. "I'd planned on a shore lunch all along so I have all the necessary stuff with me. When I realized there was nothing in this cottage in the way of food I decided to stay here and cook us both some trout." One eyebrow rose in a question. "Is that okay? Almost freezing to death is hard on the body. You need fuel to get warm again."

At that precise moment my stomach rumbled and I said the only thing I could think to say. "That sounds wonderful." Memories of shore lunches with my grandfather brought tears to my eyes but I blinked them away as I wondered at what age I'd forgotten my love of trout streams. And now I had one mere yards from my front door and a fly fisherman in front of me, reminding me of how the summer could go.

I found myself looking forward to a delicious meal and an hour later I groaned in ecstasy as I pushed away from the table replete with the remains of a shore lunch. During that hour across the table from one another we'd learned a bit about each other because what else would two strangers talk about?

"Susanna Brown." From everywhere because my father's climbing of the corporate ladder had required several moves. And as we ate that delicious trout I explained that I was taking a hiatus from work to upgrade my skills which was why I was in Southfork. I didn't mention that I'd quit my job in a snit of frustration. He didn't need to know that.

"Royce Adamson and I've lived in Southfork all my life." He also mentioned that he was single, a fact I shouldn't have cared about and did. "I make furniture and ship it everywhere." He tipped his head in a direction that I presumed was downtown Southfork. "My workshop is next to the general store."

"Where's the grocery store? I need to do some shopping." Yes he was gorgeous but other things were also important. Like eating.

He frowned. "Groceries? You should have stopped at a big box store on your way here."

"I didn't think to do so."

Another frown. "The general store doesn't carry groceries because people around here shop in real towns. You know, the kinds of places with enough people to support an actual grocery store."

I groaned. "I hope they have something that'll get me through the next few days." Until I was unpacked and had my bearings and could go elsewhere. "Because I don't even have a box of crackers."

His eyes – brown with tiny flecks of gold now that I was close enough to see – were sympathetic. "Some of the ladies in town get together to make a grocery run once a week but I think they went yesterday so they won't go for a while."

"I can drive." I'd got to Southfork by myself, hadn't I?

His head tilted a bit. "I don't go with the ladies. I take my truck, most of us bachelors do, and I go shopping whenever I need enough stuff to make the trip worthwhile. More efficient than weekly." I guessed that kind of shopping might be a guy thing as he continued. "I'm running out of a lot of stuff so it's about time to go again. If I go tomorrow, want to ride along? The truck will hold both of our stuff."

I started to let him know I was perfectly capable of driving a few miles to another town when I realized I didn't know where that town was or which direction I'd have to take to reach it. I kind of folded into myself. "I'll appreciate the ride."

He nodded. "In the meantime what say you visit me for dinner? It'll be better than starving." I'd not be able to eat a decent meal until that shopping trip. Or to eat anything at all. "My spaghetti is to die for and it's on the menu tonight."

My shoulders sagged as I realized I was about to once more be in this gorgeous man's debt. Okay, maybe not everyone would think he was gorgeous but I did. The physique. The outdoorsy vibe. The general air of competence. "Thanks." Then I asked, "Where do you live? How can I find your house?"

"It's the white two-story building behind my workshop which is next to the general store."

"Can you give me specific directions?"

His eyes went wide. Then he threw his head back and laughed. It was a deep, belly laugh and it was beautiful. "You definitely are from the city, aren't you?"

"Why? What did I say?"

"In Southfork you don't ask for specific directions. Instead you ask what the house looks like and where it is in a general sort of way. Then you simply stand in the middle of the street and look around until you see it." He finished with, "The town is that small. You can see it all from that one spot in the center of town." He thought over his words. "Though to be honest it's not actually a town. Southfork is a village." He thought still more. "Not even a village. A hamlet, maybe?" He scowled because even that wasn't right.

I finished for him. "A crossroads?"

His face cleared. "Yep, that's what Southfork is. A crossroads and one of the loveliest places on Earth."

"I agree," I said slowly remembering the trees meeting over that rippling creek and the sunshine and the tiny, quaint cottage that would be mine for as long as I chose.

We cleaned up the lunch dishes and then Royce left so I could unpack. But before leaving, he dug into his supplies and handed me a box of cookies and some grapes. "I brought them for snacks but I think you need them more than I do." He saluted as he headed for the door. "So I'll leave you to settle in." He glanced about. "In this tiny cottage it shouldn't take long."

He was right. Everything was put away in less than an hour during which I'd also made a mini-office in a corner using a wobbly table that had been on the back porch that was usable with a block of wood under one leg to stabilize it. I arranged my things on the top with my laptop precisely in the center. A perfect setting for upgrading my skill sets through online courses. Then I set about finding the internet connection the ad for the cottage had promised so I could sign up for those courses.

I didn't find it.

Maybe Royce Adamson could help. I decided to ask when I went to his place for a dinner that, now that I thought about it, would be very welcome. I finished the snacks and looked forward to tomorrow's shopping expedition when I could fill my cupboard with food.

In jeans and a comfortable shirt and wearing a jacket and sneakers that wouldn't sink into the soft earth I spent the hours until that meal outside. I checked out the creek that I now treated with respect from a safe distance. The fields stretching away and into the distance that were dotted with trees and bushes budding out in the warm sun. In mere days, if the sun continued hot, the area would be a green paradise.

I walked the length of the crossroads or town or whatever it was and checked out the few stores, lingering in the single tourist-oriented one and talking with the owner, a solid looking woman who was at home in this rural environment and who informed me I'd sadly misread the ad if I thought it meant the internet connection was dependable.

"Southfork does have high-speed internet so the ad was truthful," she said over her glasses after introducing herself as Lottie. "We have internet when whatever it is that makes it work actually functions and the wind is from the right direction. It's good enough for most of us because we're pretty laid-back around here. If it doesn't work on Monday, maybe it will on Tuesday. Or next week."

My heart sank. "What about those who need a reliable connection?"

She laughed. "They either pay a fortune or figure out something else to do with their time." Even without checking I knew I couldn't afford dependable service. So how was I to take those online classes? My heart sank as I feared I'd have to say good-bye to both my upskill ambitions and those professional friendships I'd carefully nurtured and planned to continue online so they could help me land a job when I was ready to reenter the world of work.

One thing went well during my explorations. Royce had told the truth about finding his house – or any house – easily by standing in the center of town and looking around. His was clean and neat and larger than expected. It had been built for a family instead of a bachelor and was placed a short distance behind an equally neat workshop and beneath old trees with spreading branches with what might be a garden plot behind it though it was still too early in the year for it to be more than a black rectangle enclosed by a ten-foot-high fence.

He answered on the first knock. "Don't bother to knock next time. Just come inside and holler. If I'm home, I'll answer. If not I'm in the shop. Or somewhere." Wearing snug-fitting jeans and an equally snug-fitting tee shirt, but barefoot. For some reason the combination did things to my insides that I tried to ignore and hoped he didn't notice.

To cover my embarrassment, I blurted out the first thing that came to my mind. A question. "Why do you have a high fence around your garden?"

He laughed again. "Deer can jump anything under ten feet and those veggies I work so hard for all summer are for me instead of a bunch of greedy deer."

"Oh." My face turned red as he enjoyed the fact that he knew this little piece of rural knowledge that I clearly didn't. Deer could be pests.

His hand at the small of my back turned my insides to jelly and propelled me through the hallway and to the kitchen where a table was set for two and a pot of spaghetti sauce simmered on the stove. Darn the man, anyway, what gave him the right to be so perfect?

As the incredible smell hit me, I salivated and hoped he wouldn't go through some kind of rural initiation ceremony before we could eat. Because I suddenly realized I was starved.

He didn't insist on any rituals that delayed dinner and his spaghetti lived up to his earlier boast. When I couldn't eat another bite no matter how much I wanted to I came up for air and conversation. And questions about internet access.

"How far away is the nearest town with internet access?" Because I'd figured a solution to my internet conundrum. "I need it, I can't afford it here and so must drive somewhere else and sit in my car to do online classes." I explained about the upskilling and that the ad for the rental said there was internet access.

He shoved his chair back and balanced on two legs with his entire body aligned and relaxed as he considered me. Those brown and gold eyes took me in from top to bottom and side to side and I once more hoped he didn't notice how he affected me. "Obviously you need more internet access than most people around here."

"So how far do I have to drive to get it?"

"Eighty miles more or less." I groaned and would have dropped my head to the table and pounded it a few times if I was alone but even without such a gesture it was obvious I was unhappy. He considered me still more. "I have excellent access through a wonderful and very expensive satellite provider. I need it in my business because my customers are all over the country. I'll be happy to share. No charge because we are neighbors."

"You'd do that?" My eyes went wide as I carefully didn't ask what my share would cost if I paid because I undoubtedly couldn't afford it. "Really?"

"It'll be nice to know I'm finally getting my money's worth." He pointed through the window. "It's in the shop, though, so you'll have to share space with a lot of wood."

"Sawdust?" My laptop wouldn't like that.

"My computer is in the office, and I keep the door tightly closed and there's an air filtration system." His head tipped much like it had when he was fly-fishing. "It's a rather large office. Space won't be a problem."

"If you'll let me know what hours you're open I'll make sure to be there during those hours and finish well before quitting time."

He held up a finger and shook it at me. "Remember what I said? No one in Southfork locks their doors so you can follow whatever schedule you choose." He thought a moment. "Besides, I don't have regular hours. What if the trout are biting or the garden needs tending?" He finished with, "I refuse to be a slave to a clock or calendar." A decided snort said what he thought of schedules.

"Oh." What else was there to say? And why couldn't I come up with a better response than that single, innocuous word? And why did I have the feeling my well-planned life was about to spin out of control in this tiny hamlet that was home to one of the best-looking men I'd ever seen and where the trout bit when they felt like it and life was lived in a way and on a schedule I could hardly imagine?

Chapter 3

We went shopping the next day. I bought way more than I expected to use in an entire month and ignored Royce's almost smile at the amount. I knew he politely wasn't mentioning that I'd figured out that when you live in the country you stock up when you can and you buy a lot because you don't want to be caught out with an empty cupboard if something unforeseen happens.

But eventually he couldn't keep silent any longer so he pretended a love of cooking was why I bought so much. "You must like to cook." Then he added in a voice low enough that he hoped I wouldn't hear, "Country living isn't like in the city. No stores open twenty-four seven if you forgot something." He smiled brightly, thinking I'd not heard as he put still another of my purchases in his truck.

I matched his bright smile with one of my own and ignored the remark about stocking up, choosing instead to let him think I'd only heard the bit about cooking. "I do like to cook but the results definitely aren't gourmet." The only truthful thing I could say because my kitchen skills would never match his excellent spaghetti.

Then something occurred to me. "Speaking of which, I owe you a meal. Two meals, actually. Lunch and dinner." Because that's what he'd given me. A shore lunch and a spaghetti dinner. "What about lunch tomorrow at my place?" Surely I could come up with something to equal that lunch. I'd brought a cookbook. There must be recipes in it somewhere that even a mediocre cook like me could master and I'd figure out the second meal later.

He considered the offer. "Okay but you must take into consideration that the trout are hitting. So what say I stop by as soon as I catch my limit?"

My brain was already working on a menu that could come even close to his fresh fish lunch so it took a moment to realize what he'd said. He was willing to come only *after* he caught his limit? Really? And when was that likely to be?

More to the point, what could I serve that could wait for him to finish fishing and still be edible? I almost barfed at the challenge but I wasn't about to let him know I was panicking because maybe this was how small towns worked and I'd just have to adapt.

As I tried to figure out menus and how to avoid him seeing how he was affecting me because I'd not only have to cook a few meals for him, I'd have to sit across the table from him while we ate and then again while I worked in his shop, his eyes narrowed. "Speaking of fishing, you said you fly fish."

I nodded and he continued. "Do you have a rod?" I shook my head and he continued, "I have several and an extra creel." Of course he did, all dedicated fly fishermen do. My grandfather had six. That I knew of.

"But it's way too cold still to go wading with bare

feet and the shore is unreliable – as you learned yesterday – so you shouldn't fish from there. You might want to get a pair of waders while we're here." He finished with, "There's a sporting goods store in the next block." Then he added, "If you want to do some fishing while you're here."

We headed for that sporting goods store and when we exited I had a pair of waders plus an assortment of warm things to wear with and inside them because though the sun was doing its best there was still snow in shaded places and the creek would still be icy.

"Want to practice casting before we head to the creek?" he asked a few days later after a lunch of hamburgers grilled on the ancient grill that came with my cottage because I'd decided I could cook them after he arrived, whenever that would be, so they'd be fresh when we ate and even I couldn't mess up hamburgers.

The meal was a success. I felt like I'd passed a test though I wasn't sure if it was a rural life test or one to determine if I was fit to become a Royce Adamson groupie. "Want to practice a few dry land casts before we head for the creek?" He added, "The trees meet overhead over the creek and it can be tricky to get your line where you want it without getting it stuck in a branch."

"Yes, please." I spoke in a small voice, remembering my grandfather and my childhood. The streams I'd fished with my grandfather had been wide open. No trees anywhere. "I need the practice. It's been years."

We found an open spot behind the cottage in one of those fields that seemed to go on forever. He watched as I pulled a length of line from the reel, dropped it to the ground beside me and tried to remember everything I'd been taught. My mouth went dry as I sent out my first cast. It was a disaster and I was glad for the open field.

But it didn't take long to regain the rhythm of fly fishing and soon Royce decreed my ability equal to his. It was a nice lie but I felt adequate to the creek and the huge, ancient trees that overarched it. So we pulled on our waders and headed for the icy waters of the quiet south fork of the white-water river that came from an unknown place beyond the other side of town and that, after passing my quaint cottage, headed out towards some other equally unknown place far, far away.

Royce pointed out a likely spot for me before moving far enough downstream that our lines wouldn't become tangled. I proceeded to cast, watching him covertly during that quiet moment while my fly rested on the water before starting to reel it in, and that was how I figured out what was truly behind his choice of a spot for me.

The bottom of the creek where I stood was level with a sandy bottom. Totally safe. Royce, on the other hand, stood among rocks and threaded his way carefully along an uneven, gravelly creek bed. The man was making sure I'd not end up head first in the cold water as when we'd met while he fished the more dangerous rocky portion. Which also happened to be the most likely spot to find trout.

I didn't know whether to laugh or cry. When we took a break, I let him know I'd seen through his tactic. "It's a good thing we didn't bet on who'll catch the most trout."

"What are you talking about?"

"You gave yourself the premier spot. If we'd have made a bet, I'd lose."

His face turned pink but he didn't look away. "It's also the most difficult spot on the creek to walk. It's not actually safe." The pink became red. "I was considering your safety."

"Or you wanted to catch the most trout. But I'm letting you know that the time I fell in the creek was an anomaly. I'm usually able to navigate difficult terrain just fine."

"Then when we go back to the creek, we'll switch places."

So we did and I soon wished I'd kept silent because he was right. The rocky bottom was treacherous and I spent so much time being careful not to fall that I caught nothing, not one single trout, while Royce caught his limit.

His grin when we compared catches was infuriating and I'd have said something except I'd asked for it. He shut his creel with a satisfied snap. "Up for another trout lunch?" I nodded and he asked, "Your place or mine?"

"You have a better kitchen." Which he did, the large, white house having been designed for a family with a kitchen that could feed a passel of assorted kids plus numerous relatives and a half dozen or so neighbors.

He agreed. "The cottage is just that. A cottage. A pretty place beside the creek but it was never intended to be a year-around home so no reason for a decent kitchen." Or decent much of anything else, I thought, considering what I now knew was a pretty, quaint, and fairly decrepit cottage in the country. But I loved it in spite of the mice, the wind blowing through cracks in the walls and all the other things that were less than perfect.

Halfway through our lunch, I thought of something. "Does this mean I still owe you two meals because, even though I made one lunch, I haven't yet had you over for dinner and now this lunch adds still another meal to my debt?"

"We both worked on this meal so this one is a draw. You only owe me one meal and I intend to hold you to it."

Preparing the lunch had been an oddly intimate thing with Royce showing me where everything was located and the two of us working in tandem as if we'd done it a thousand times before. There was an element of warmth and something else I couldn't describe added to his pure, unadulterated, sex appeal.

But the meal debt needed to be dealt with. I spoke before I could chicken out. "Tomorrow night." Then I took a deep breath and added, hoping I wasn't displaying a total lack of small-town etiquette by mentioning a specific time. "And it doesn't matter what a bunch of fish are doing. Be at the cottage at six sharp." I frowned sternly. "No later, whether the trout are biting or not." And I waited for him to argue with my cavalier disregard of his non-schedule by telling me where to go.

Instead, he said, "Yes ma'am."

"No argument?"

"No ma'am."

He sighed hugely at my surprise and explained. "My momma taught me never to argue with a woman when she gives an actual order in a particular tone of voice. The tone of voice you just used. Momma told me to say 'yes ma'am' and do whatever I'm told to do." His pained expression said it might be hard to follow that advice. "Even if the trout are biting."

I laughed. Couldn't help it. Soon he was laughing with me and I followed him to his back porch that overlooked a yard that was fuzzy green with early spring grass and a garden that was still a black rectangle. He examined that black space. "Want to share my garden? I might have been a bit overly ambitious when I made it so big. I'll never use the full space."

"I suppose so." But honesty is a virtue. "I've never gardened before."

"Why not?"

"Never lived where we could have one." A deficit of having an ambitious father. Choose a house near work to cut commute time with the resulting small to nonextant yard and my grandparent's country garden was always planted by the time I visited.

"No garden?" He whistled in surprise but recovered quickly. "Well, if you're up for it, it's easy enough. What do you want to grow?" I didn't know. "Tomatoes? Beans? Squash?"

"Those sound ominous. And difficult." Best to remind him I was a beginner. "Whatever's easiest."

He blinked. "Radishes in the spring." He'd probably never heard of a beginner gardener because everyone in small towns knows how to grow things, it being a sacred part of their heritage. "When we see how well you do with radishes, we'll decide on other veggies for later."

The silence lengthened and that feeling I got

whenever I was near him increased exponentially. It wasn't uncomfortable, though, and it was evolving into something different from that first time I'd seen him. Instead of being firmly planted beneath the sun and earth and sky I felt as if I was suspended between two strange, unexplored worlds and I didn't know which was the real one, the world of today that included Royce or some other, unknown one. It was an odd feeling, one I'd never experienced and I knew at last what people meant when they said they'd lost touch with reality. He affected me that much.

"Thanks for the fishing and the lunch." I prepared to leave before I made a fool of myself.

Those brown-gold eyes turned to me. The gold flecks I'd never seen in anyone else, ever, were bright in the brown depths. "It's early yet. Why don't you bring your computer and stuff over to the shop now and we can carve out a spot for you?"

Then those brown-gold eyes darkened while the gold flecks grew brighter. He leaned against the porch rail in what was outwardly a casual way but in some way I couldn't figure wasn't casual at all as my breath left me because somehow I knew those worlds I was suspended between were about to get even more complicated.

As I turned to go get my things to bring back to his shop he straightened and took a step towards me. He took my hand in his and turned me around so instead of my leaving we faced one another. Then he wrapped his free hand around my neck and gently pulled me towards him. And kissed me.

Chapter 4

Not a deep kiss, not exactly romantic, but not platonic either. I found myself responding in kind while wondering why we were standing there like a couple of idiots and kissing in a way that could mean anything -- or nothing -- while also wondering in some remote corner of my mind were I'd be when it ended. Which world I'd find myself in.

He released me. "Need help bringing stuff to the shop?" And the everyday world returned, completely normal and spring warm and smelling like blossoms and new grass. The world as if he hadn't just kissed me.

And how could that be when the earth had shifted and the universe had just changed in some fundamental way as we kissed? Surely the after-kiss world couldn't be the same as the before-kiss one. Could it?

But it was.

How depressing.

I breathed a shuddering breath and took myself in hand. What was I thinking?! What was with all my idiotic thoughts about shifting worlds when nothing had actually happened? Nothing cosmic, anyway. It had merely been a kiss and I'd been caught off guard. That was all. One kiss. Just one casual kiss. No big deal. I shrugged it off. Tried to shrug it off. "I don't have a lot of stuff. I can handle it but thanks for the offer."

He pointed to a garden cart near the black rectangle at the back of the yard. "You can use that. It should hold everything so you can do it in one trip." He levered away from the porch, retrieved the cart, and led me to the front of his house where I took the handle from him.

Then he kissed me again. Unlike after that first kiss, though, this time he acknowledged that we'd kissed. He grinned widely. But I didn't know what to make of that broad smile any more than I'd known what to make of the first kiss that he hadn't acknowledged in any way. It was all very disconcerting.

But I'm not a coward. I didn't look away. In fact, I met him look for look and so I read that those brown-gold eyes were just a tiny bit flustered. Was that devilish grin hiding the fact that his world had also been upended? Impossible to tell but I had a moment of satisfaction – and hope -- because he deserved to have his world as totally upended as mine.

As I turned to leave I managed to act normal. I gathered what dignity I could find and pulled the empty cart past a few houses, across the stone bridge over the creek and then down the slight incline to the tiny cottage beside the trout stream where I stood for a long time and breathed deeply until the world righted itself. It might not be a different world but, wanted or not, it was the one in which must function.

I stomped about and reminded myself that I was a competent person. I loaded my computer and printer and a bunch of notebooks into the cart along with everything else I might need and brought it all back to the workshop beside the general store while trying to figure how to act during all those future hours I'd be spending in that space while Royce worked in the shop. Meeting him look for look would be a good start but it wouldn't keep me sane forever.

When I got there Royce, of course, acted as if nothing had happened. No kiss. No world changing event. Because as far as he was concerned nothing had happened? Because he hadn't been affected in the least and I'd been wrong to think otherwise?

With a sigh I decided that was probably it and I'd better get signed up for those online classes if I wanted the bright future I'd mapped out for myself and forget the future my imagination was already inventing that would take place in this crossroads town I'd not known existed until I saw that ad in the paper. An imaginary life that included the man who was giving me goosebumps but who didn't seem interested in sharing anything beyond a couple casual kisses, a love of fly fishing and a garden.

Oh well.

Over the next week as I took over a fair-sized piece of his office and set up my computer and all those notebooks, things somehow went well. And I learned how gardening was done.

Royce tilled the soil. I planted radishes while he planted things I didn't recognize because they were only seeds of various sizes and colors. We both pulled weeds and tossed them into a compost pile and watered everything equally and hoped for the best. Royce explained how to check the sky for rain but I never did get how it worked. The sky was just the sky, not a blue weather forecasting machine.

I started searching for online classes. AI was at the top of my list of things to master but statistics was up there too so I'd be able to rattle off important-sounding numbers to potential future employers.

Royce, who was watching with interest and a mystified expression, questioned the logic of my plan. "Isn't the corporate world in something of a depression? Lots of empty buildings and so on?"

I sighed and agreed. "But corporate America is what I know and the economy will revive."

"Small businesses are the backbone of the economy. Not just corporations."

"There aren't a lot of classes for truly small businesses because they don't employ a lot of people and by the time they get large enough to employ enough people to justify creating a class for them they are no longer small."

"I see your point. I have no employees so there's no reason for nonexistent people to learn woodworking though I could certainly use a bit of extra help when things get busy. Like now."

"Good for you. Your business is expanding."

He shuddered. "I hope not."

"I thought all businesses want to grow larger."

"If I had to figure how to keep employees busy and spend my day solving problems instead of making furniture and couldn't close down when the trout are biting I think I'd die. I'd rather walk barefoot on cut glass." His eyes showed true horror at the thought.

He glanced through the list of classes I'd highlighted. "AI? Really? And sales and marketing strategies of the future? Looks like you don't plan to stay in Southfork."

"I never thought about it one way or another. Though, now that you mention it, living here would be like grabbing a little slice of heaven."

He leaned against the oversized desk in his office where he managed orders and other details of Adamson Furniture and he did it in a way that made me lose my breath. It was what he did when he wanted to think something through and my breath stopped every single time. Every. Single. Time. "All that stuff you are learning is for big businesses in big cities. Too much hassle for me. Too many problems." He sighed. "I'd rather go fishing."

"What if you get busy enough to need employees?"

"Should that day ever come I'll make sure to hire people who know what's truly important."

"Like trout?"

"Yep."

"Are your orders ever late because of fishing?"

"Of course not." His snort said he was insulted that I could even suggest such a thing. "I only take as many orders as I know I can handle. With or without fishing."

"So your business is stuck being small and so is your income."

"My income is taking off like a house on fire."

"How so?"

"Whenever I get so busy that I can't handle my orders, I raise my prices. When that happens the orders slow down for a while but eventually they pick up again at the more expensive level." He smiled the smile of someone who knew their worth. "So I stay exactly as busy as I wish but my income keeps rising."

"So you're not likely to ever need help."

"Hmmmmm." He tipped his head in thought.

"Actually, I'd love to employ someone who truly wants to live in Southfork and has excellent business skills and likes to fish. Someone like you."

"You don't know what my skills are."

"I'm sure they are excellent and whatever they are will prove useful."

I didn't know what to say. Silence filled the room and grew until it was suffocating and someone had to say something and since he just stood and leaned against that huge desk and waited for me to make the first move I finally couldn't stand it any longer and asked a question. "Are you offering me a job?"

He examined me for a long time. Up and down and sidewise. I felt that examination in every piece of my body. "Maybe. Are you interested?"

"Maybe. Tell me more."

He pulled a chair beside mine and dropped into it and checked over the potential classes on my list. "Nothing about using a lathe or a router so you'd not be much use in the shop. But bookkeeping is always useful." He peered closer and a chuckle began somewhere deep in his belly as he read the next class on my list. "But as for the AI stuff do you truly want to learn how to argue with a robot?"

"AI is the big thing now. Without AI skills I'll never get a job should I leave Southfork."

"So don't leave Southfork." He shuddered. "Tell you what, Susanna. You come to work for me for a while. I'll pay you something and we'll see if we can put those wonderful skills to work so you can stay a while in Southfork. If you want to stay, that is."

I didn't know I was going to say it until the words came out. "I want to stay." Then honesty compelled me to add, "For a while. I think."

Another chuckle was followed by, "But this offer comes with a caveat."

"What kind of caveat?"

"When the trout are biting, we stop work and go fishing. Both of us. Together. And we share the cooking when the day ends and we enjoy a fish dinner. Same goes for gardening. If the garden needs tending that becomes part of the job."

I found myself putting my hand out. "Deal."

He took it. "Deal and I'm stunned. I actually have an employee. I never thought that would happen and it wouldn't if you didn't like fishing." I silently thanked my grandfather for the hours spent in the stream that ran along the back of his property.

"When do I start and what will I be doing?"

He scratched his head. "Darned if I know. Whenever you think."

"What time should I arrive?" I'd show up tomorrow and I'd be on time even if he wasn't because that would show him I was a competent employee.

"After you finish breakfast whenever that is but don't come tomorrow."

"Why not?"

"Before you get busy with a new job you should take some time and get to know Southfork. The place you're considering as a semi-permanent home. Go for a walk. Meet some people. Check out the swimming beach. There are benches built into the stone bridge over the creek that runs past your place that are great for just sitting and enjoying the day. And when you think you have a feel for what Southfork is like, come back here and kind of hang around and eventually there'll be something that needs doing that you can do."

I didn't know whether to laugh or cry. It was utterly the most ridiculous job interview I'd ever experienced. I shut my laptop and wondered what I'd gotten myself into. But I couldn't stop the inner warmth that crept through me as I thought ahead to the coming summer. My rural laid-back grandfather would approve though my ambitious father wouldn't understand.

He'd still love me, of course, but he'd shake his head and say I'd taken leave of my senses. He'd worked hard to give his family the kind of life that work and dedication could provide and his business classes had made it possible. He'd understand my taking online classes but not how anyone connected to him could even remotely consider fishing as part of paid employment.

I wanted to honor both my grandfather and my father so I decided that even though I was going to work for Royce and didn't need any classes, I'd sign up for a few. Doing so would prevent my father from having a heart attack and if staying in Southfork didn't work out, I'd have those skills to fall back on when I left the tiny crossroads and returned to the real world.

Because one thing my brief interview had shown me was that Southfork wasn't the real world. Not if jobs there included weeding gardens and fishing when the trout were biting. The ultimate truth, though, after much thought, was that it probably was part of someone's real world but it was its own tiny world within that weird world. It truly was an anomaly, a place of rural beauty and slow living and people who knew one another.

I liked that. I could call it home. Maybe. For a

while. Longer, if things worked out.

Considering my vow to keep my father happy I asked Royce if I could still use his internet once I was an employee. I explained about my father and his eyes crinkled that families were strange but we had to love them anyway and surely, if mothers were to be listened to, then fathers should be also.

"Take as many classes as you want and use the internet all you want, even during working hours if there's nothing that needs doing at the moment because, as you already know, I don't believe in schedules."

He thought for a few seconds. "Besides, what you'll be doing with those classes is called upskilling and that should be a part of any good employee package. So I'll pay for the classes. Up to a point." His lips pursed. "But I won't pay for AI because I see no need for robots with encyclopedic knowledge who don't know the first thing about making furniture or how to know what customers want when said customers don't know themselves."

A statement that told me why Royce's furniture business was so successful and would continue to get better over time. The man cared about both his craft and his customers.

Chapter 5

I learned Royce meant every word about how our working relationship would be and I learned it my first day on the job after the day spent elsewhere getting to know Southfork and I learned because the fish were biting. When I showed up bright and early in neat, gray slacks and a print shirt I hoped would pass for business casual in a small town on this, the first day of my new job -- the day before having been spent wandering through fields and along country roads -- well, when I stepped inside, the shop was empty.

I dropped into a chair at the oversize desk we'd share that I'd earlier discovered was a huge, repurposed table with drawers added below and shelves above. I would wait politely for him to arrive and introduce me to my job.

Then I noticed the handwritten note on the desk.

The note said the fish were biting so he was gone and I should do whatever I wished. Find something to do in the office that might be considered furniture related. Or start on those online classes. Or go somewhere other than the shop because it was a lovely day and such days shouldn't be wasted. Or do whatever

I felt like doing that was positive in nature.

According to the note, whatever I did would be fine with him and would be considered work related because even if it didn't have to do specifically with furniture it surely would help make me a better person and by extension a better employee.

So, after thinking through the many possible connotations of such a concept, I turned on my computer and signed up for three online classes and felt righteous and proud of making good use of time spent without my boss' supervision. I wondered if he'd agree that I'd help move the business forward through my chosen upskilling classes.

I was already proficient in bookkeeping but advanced courses never hurt so that was my first choice. I wasn't so sure about a course in marketing because he already had more orders than he could handle but it could prove useful if that changed so that skill, too, could be a plus for the business.

I sincerely doubted learning how to negotiate contracts advantageously would be helpful but it looked easy and my father would approve so I signed up for that, too, and decided I'd offer to pay for that one myself because it wasn't related to woodworking while knowing that Royce would insist on paying for it because that's the kind of guy he was.

How did I know he was that kind of guy? I debated the idea as I shut off the computer after filling in the last bit of required information for the upcoming classes and closed it against any dust that might infiltrate the tightly closed office. Those chores accomplished I wondered what to do next because of course he wouldn't return until the fish stopped biting or he caught his limit. Either could be a while and the day stretched ahead.

As I thought about the coming day, a Bluebird chanced to pass the open window and I followed its flight. Was it going for a visit because it was too lovely a day to spend looking for insects? Had it been talking with Royce and learned the value of living in the moment? As it disappeared from view and I thought about Bluebirds and happiness I remembered the third suggestion in Royce's note. Go for a walk. Another day, another walk.

So that's what I did.

Lottie wasn't busy in the only store in Southfork that carried anything a tourist might possibly want. "Not many tourists come here," she said without rancor. "But when they do, I'm here and they are usually glad of it." She was, of course, sitting in a chair just outside the open door where she'd be able to quickly respond should a customer come along. In the meantime she could enjoy the time between sales.

I was curious. "How do you make a viable business out of what must be merely occasional sales?"

She rose so we were eye to eye. "This is Southfork, dearie. Rent is cheap, owning is even cheaper if you bought long ago, which I did. So my costs are low and I like meeting people so it works for me." She examined the sidewalk that was currently empty of tourists though a car was approaching from the highway, throwing dust behind it. "Of course, people vary. There are natives and there are tourists. They are different and I never forget it"

My face must have shown a question because she answered without the question being asked. She pointed to the car that turned into the tiny town and pulled to a stop in front of her store. "Those are tourists." She smiled broadly and rose from her chair to attend to them. I was sure they would enjoy their visit to Southfork and that Lottie would enjoy talking with them.

As she pulled the chair to one side to wait while she took care of her customers, she said softly, "You, dearie, are not a tourist. You are a native because you are renting Mrs. Sanders' cottage and because Royce Adamson likes you and hired you." Then she shooed the tourists into her store.

Royce had only hired me a couple days earlier. The Southfork rumor mill was clearly efficient. But it was the 'likes you' part that made my insides turn as warm as the summer sun made my face flush. Lottie noticed as she followed the tourists into her store and preened a bit as if proud of her contribution to a budding romance but she said nothing as I followed and wandered the aisles with her watching from behind the counter as if she'd been there all along like a good business person attending to her store.

When I approached the counter with a cute sweatshirt that said Southfork on the front, she rang up my purchase, followed soon after by a rather hefty sale from the tourists who said how lovely the town was and also the river with the stone bridge where they planned to have a picnic lunch.

There were a few other stores in Southfork plus a gas station. One of the stores was a feed store that turned out to be the social hub of the town, a fact I soon learned. Another was a hardware store that was also a farm equipment store with what seemed like acres of farm machinery both inside and spread out outside across the front, side and back.

The back was where used equipment was on display. That was where a couple ancient men and a youngish woman in overalls were examining tractors while chugging pop from one of the two vending machines in front. The other vending machine contained an assortment of candy and chips.

I chose pop and chips and didn't know where to go next. Check out feed for cattle and pigs in the feed store and meet and possibly talk with the residents of Southfork, pretend to admire a bunch of confusing farm machinery, or go beyond town and explore the fields and small wooded lots that were so close to the horizon they appeared to float in the azure blue sky? A difficult choice.

The decision was made for me. As I stood to one side of the street that was the main street of town, someone behind me cleared their throat. I turned and found myself staring at Royce, complete with rod, creel with a pair of waders slung over one shoulder. "The trout were biting. I caught my limit early."

"So we can get to work?"

He examined that blue sky, shading his eyes with one hand and reminding me of that first glimpse of him in the creek bordering my back yard. Then he was poetry in motion. Now he was a Greek statue except for the waders over his shoulder and the way his eyes crinkled as that early summer sun gave him another layer of tan.

He mused, "It's a lovely day." I waited to find out what that meant in terms of work. "Too lovely to spend indoors." He examined me much as he'd done the sky.

"What say we go for a walk instead and consider it therapy?" He took my arm. "Isn't that what corporations do? Pay tons of money for someone to come and tell employees how to be happy?" He gestured to the sky. "This will do just as well and is free."

"How'd you know I was thinking of going for a walk?"

"Easy. Look at that sky. Anyone who'd choose to be inside on a day like today when there is any alternative must be missing a brain." He indicated the fishing equipment draped over his body. "If you can wait while I get rid of this stuff I can show you some of the really special places in the area." He considered the creel at his waist. "And when we return we can have another shore lunch. Or dinner. Depends on how long we're gone." His eyes narrowed in a question. "Unless you're tired of fish dinners."

"Never." Which was true thanks to that grandfather who loved to fish as much as Royce did.

"Wait here," he said and took off towards his house at a fast trot. He returned minutes later without the fishing gear but wearing a backpack. "Sustenance in the form of whatever I could find that qualified as portable food and drink plus a sheet to sit on if there's no grass so you can keep that oh-so-professional business outfit clean."

I examined my dress casual outfit. "I wasn't sure what to wear."

He shook his head. "Whatever you grab. This isn't the city and my business is mail order. I've never had a customer show up in person and I've never figured out how to do a virtual meet and greet so I don't dress for the camera." His face was wry. "Which is probably just as well because I'm normally covered in sawdust."

He first led me to the stone bridge over the river that ran beside my cottage. The tourists were already there and we talked a bit. They loved the ambiance of the place and the water foaming over the rocks that water foamed over and they enthused over the trout flashing brightly in the clear creek. Then they finished their lunch and left.

Royce and I were alone and the silence grew large and lasted forever without being awkward because there was so much to see and appreciate that it seemed like hardly any time had elapsed when Royce gently took my arm and led me back into the sun filled day and we headed for fields beyond town that were now spring green with yellow flowers scattered everywhere.

To me, everything was the same. Fields, flowers, trees and such. Royce saw it differently. "We stay away from the Rhodes' farm. Cows and cow patties, plus a bull if you get in the wrong pasture." We skirted the Rhodes' place and another he said belonged to someone from a city somewhere who never visited. "Lots of thistles. He ignores the letters from the county agent to get rid of them."

So we avoided that field, too, though it was lovely because even invasive thistles belong in a picture. "There." He pointed. "That's the place. Belongs to Lottie. She gave up farming a while back and her fields are going back to nature until she decides what to do next. A farmer cuts it for hay but it's not high enough yet so it should be good for a picnic." At which moment my stomach rumbled.

We found a spot beneath a tree of some unknown

variety and spread the sheet over what turned out to be soft grass. Soon we were both lying on that sheet beneath a tree that was fully leafed out though the leaves were still spring green and staring up at the dappled sky.

I thought we'd eat immediately. I was wrong. As I examined that sky and decided there was no place I'd rather be at that moment, I rolled slightly to see Royce better. What I saw decided me we weren't ready to eat. Because he was asleep.

Chapter 6

I was okay with that because it gave me the chance to study him without being embarrassed. The way his hair didn't do what some barber wanted it to and kept flopping across his forehead. The sun creases at the corners of his eyes. The way his chest rose and fell as he breathed and why that should send shivers through me I couldn't figure. But it did.

I considered the totality of the man on the ground beside me, comfortable in his own skin and his place in the world. I didn't know very many people as okay with themselves and their world as Royce Adamson and I found that fact, too, to be stunningly seductive.

I sucked in my breath as the knowledge hit me like a sledge hammer that he was becoming more important to me than I'd have thought possible when I first saw him in waders in the creek that first day and that day I'd thought him so perfect that I'd actually believed him to be a figment of my imagination. Now, somehow, he was more important than any other man ever.

I rolled away in stunned surprise at my feelings and stared at the grass beyond the sheet. What was happening? I hadn't known him long enough to be romantically interested. Had I? I didn't think so but the idea nibbled at the edge of my consciousness as I listened to the rhythm of his breathing change from that of sleep to wakefulness.

I waited for him to fully return to the world. And to me.

"Can we eat lying down?" His voice was rough with sleep. "It's perfect here and I'm too comfortable to move a single muscle and sit up."

"We can eat but drinking might prove difficult." I giggled into the grass that tickled my nose because I was close enough to the edge of the sheet to watch the green blades wave in the breeze.

"So we eat first. That'll give us enough energy to sit up and have a drink." I felt rather than heard his frown. "Though the food is in my backpack." Once more I felt rather than saw him look around for the backpack. "It's near you." I felt a hand on my shoulder. It pointed to the backpack lying among those blades of grass. "Can you reach it?"

I laughed. I couldn't help it. "I know you aren't lazy because I've seen you fishing and it must take a lot of energy to make furniture."

"I can be lazy. I know how." Unvoiced laughter was in his words. "But today is right for a picnic and the sun is warm and I'm with the most beautiful woman in the world so it's only right to take advantage of those things while also being lazy. It's perfection."

My breath stopped and I didn't know what to say but I didn't have to say anything because before I had a chance to do anything, before I could even react, he's used the hand that had been pointing to the backpack to roll me onto my back. Then he proceeded to lever himself over me, turning that dappled sunlight into shadow as his body blocked the sun. Then he kissed me.

As before, there was no passion in the kiss but it wasn't chaste either. Somewhere in between. He withdrew and those eyes with crinkles in the corners examined me. He sighed and said, "I do enjoy kissing beautiful women."

He thought a moment. "No, that's not right. Not women, plural. One woman, singular, named Susanna who happens to work for me and I think that's the most amazing thing ever." He collapsed onto his back. "Think of the opportunities our togetherness will present." He shook his head in mock thought.

Then he rose on one elbow until he could peer down at me, once more creating a shadow. "If you are of a like mind, that is. About kissing. If you like kissing guys who think you are beautiful." He frowned and shook his head. "No, that's not what I mean. Not guys, plural. Rather one guy. Me." One eyebrow rose in a question.

"Sounds good to me." If anyone had paid attention, they'd have thought I was catching a cold. My voice was that husky.

"Excellent." He almost purred and I thought he was going to kiss me again. Instead he reached over me, stretching as far as possible and pulled the backpack onto the sheet. In mere moments we were eating sandwiches and bananas while lying on our backs studying the sky and discussing the various shades of blue to be found on a bright summer day.

I did get one more kiss, a very casual one as I stuffed the remains of our lunch into his backpack as he slung the straps through his arms when, with a self-satisfied expression, he took my arm, considered the day once more, leaned over and gave me another kiss and we proceeded back the way we'd come. Towards Southfork.

I decided it had been a very nice, though somewhat confusing, couple of hours.

He shaded his eyes with one hand. "Furniture orders are piling up and, unfortunately, I can't take unlimited time off for both fishing and beautiful days. At some point in time, I must choose." He scowled. "I've already gone fishing and had an overly long lunch hour. So it's time to get to work." He sighed deeply.

We reached town. Royce looked around. "Tourists?" A Lexus was parked in front of Lottie's store, conservative dark blue and shiny even after the gravel road. "We don't usually get tourists of that class around here. Upper class, definitely. We usually see more the average, middle-class type."

I didn't know how to feel. "Not tourists." Whether to laugh or cry because I recognized the car and of course it wasn't dusty because my father's car would never dare gather dust. "That's my father."

Just then, the door to Lottie's store opened and my father exited, suit and tie intact and looking as if he'd just come from a meeting with the CEO of a Fortune 500 company. Except he was the CEO. He spied me and approached, gathering me in a hug. "Susanna."

When I surfaced, he looked me up and down. "I wasn't sure I'd find you." He looked back at Lottie's store. "People around here aren't too forthcoming and there aren't any street signs or house numbers for me to locate you that way. I thought I'd have to leave without seeing you."

Lottie followed him outside and looked him up and down. "I couldn't know you were who you said you were." She folded her arms. "And Susanna, here, is alone in that tiny cottage that a kitten could break into." She tipped her head to one side. "So of course I wouldn't say where you could find her."

My father shook his head and a deep chuckle started somewhere in his middle. "Small towns. I should have known."

"Known what?" Lottie dared him to laugh.

My father's eyes crinkled. "I grew up in a small town. I should have known better than to ask a local where to find another local." He put me away from him enough to see me better. "Though Susanna hasn't been here long enough to be considered a local. It takes at least two generations to be local." He tipped his head from one side to the other.

His head swiveled to take in Royce and his eyes narrowed. "Unless there's a connection between my daughter and someone who is local that bridges that generational gap." His eyes asked Royce if he was that connection.

Royce started to speak but I didn't give him a chance. "Dad, this is Royce Adamson. My boss."

My father's eyes went wide. "You have a job? I thought you were taking a break. Getting a few classes under your belt. That kind of thing."

"That changed."

My father's eyes said he'd like to know what brought about the change but he didn't ask, merely shook Royce's hand and nodded to Lottie as they examined him like they'd examine an exotic insect. It was understandable with the business suit and Lexus and his CEO vibe. The vibe he'd practiced when I was a kid until he got it right.

"Where's Mom?"

"Home. I was on a business trip and since I was in the area, your mother insisted I drop by for a visit." He hugged me. "I have instructions to find out every single thing that's going on in your life and report back."

At his words, Lottie relaxed and I knew my father had passed some kind of test and that word would spread through the tiny town that he was okay. A decent person in spite of the Lexus and the expensive suit. My father noticed Lottie's change of attitude and winked at me and I was glad for the small town he'd grown up in where my grandfather still resided.

My father looked around. "No café in town, right?" Lottie nodded. "Anywhere we can get a cup of coffee?" He looked from me to Lottie to Royce and we all shook our heads. "Any place we can make some ourselves?" His shoulders went up and down. "I'd prefer talking with my daughter somewhere other than the middle of the street even though this is a lovely town."

"We can go to my cottage."

Royce shook his head. "My place has a table that doesn't need to be propped up, an actual kitchen and the shop is next door if your father wants to see where you work."

My father nodded with what might have been a relieved glance at me because he knows what my homes tend to be like. I'm more into ambiance than practicality, thus the cottage that would blow away in a breeze but has a lovely creek in the back yard.

We followed Royce to his house with Royce pointing out the shop as we passed. My father's expression wondered at the small size. Of course he did, anything less than international in scope was too small for him to consider a real business. I sighed and hoped he'd not say anything.

When there was a private moment because Royce was checking out the picnic table in the back yard to see if it was suitable for someone in an obviously expensive business suit, I hugged my father. "Thank you for not looking down on my new job. Or my new boss."

He wagged his head back and forth and rolled his eyes skyward. "I'm trying to see things from your perspective but honestly, it's hard." He put me away from him so he could see my thoughts. "Is this about a job or about your boss? Because there's electricity in the air and there's no storm on the horizon."

I blushed and he noticed and answered his own question "Yep, it's the guy." He rolled his eyes again. "When I think how hard I worked to get away from the small town I grew up in and now I see my daughter returning to those same roots, I can only think that life has a warped sense of humor." But his eyes were smiling as he looked around at the kind of place he'd known as a child and left as soon as possible.

As we drank coffee at that picnic table after Royce scrubbed the bench until there was no possibility of a single speck of dirt to sully my father's suit, my father turned to me to ask the question he'd been waiting for the right moment to ask. "Tell me about your last job and why you quit."

I explained about the lack of promotions and then, in a fit of pique, I told him about the exit interview to get across that the business itself wasn't a good fit. I repeated the exit interview almost verbatim.

My father bit his lip, his eyes went dark and broody and he and Royce both went unexpectedly very still. I figured it must be a guy thing though I couldn't understand why letting a bunch of creeps know what I thought of them turned Royce's eyes dark and my father's face to granite.

"What?" I poured myself another cup of coffee from the huge thermos Royce had brought outside and added cream and sugar to turn it into my favorite drink. "I didn't like the business and I didn't like the owners. So I quit." I chewed and swallowed it. "End of story."

My father went quieter and he and Royce nodded ever so slightly as their eyes met. Then both put on smiley faces and we finished our coffee and headed across the alley to check out the furniture shop and the space where I'd be upskilling for a new job when I left Southfork but all he did was say quietly, "I'm glad you got out of there when you did."

Chapter 7

I was relieved. "I was afraid you'd say I should have showed them what I was made of, received a promotion, and left only when I could do so from a position of strength." Because that would serve me well in my next job, something my father had always emphasized about jobs and life in general.

He didn't say that. He surprised me. "Always trust your instincts. You did the right thing." Royce nodded and again I wondered what they were both thinking that they didn't say out loud.

My father was carefully noncommittal about the woodworking shop. He took a few cautious steps through the maze of machines and wood. "Nice place." Another few steps. "Neat. Clean. Organized. Good flow." I silently thanked him for finding things he could compliment even though he clearly struggled to do so.

Royce led the way to the office. "It's where Susanna works on those classes she's taking and does my bookkeeping." His next comment said he'd read the restraint behind my father's comments. "I know this isn't the kind of business you're used to. It probably looks messy to someone like you."

I loved my father for his next remark. "I grew up

on a farm. Ever been in a barn during haying season?"

Royce relaxed and that was the first I knew how tense he'd been. "Yes I have. There are lots of farmers around here and someone always needs help with haying." And just like that the two men were okay with each other and I followed them into the office to show my father what I was doing while knowing he didn't hear anything because he and Royce were too caught up in all the things that could go wrong while turning cut grass into tightly wrapped bundles of hay that needed immediate attention. Before it rained.

Which made me realize something. My father and Royce were alike in a lot of ways. The knowledge was sudden and sharp and I didn't know why it made me feel good. But it did and I hugged the feeling to me as my father finally turned back to me and asked sensible questions about the classes I was taking while telling me why they'd be useful when I returned to the normal world and applied for a job.

Royce stayed in the shop when we were done with the tour because, as he said, he'd frittered away most of the day already and probably should do something work related. But he insisted I take the rest of the day off. Maybe the rest of the week because he could handle things and fathers didn't visit often enough to waste precious visiting time with mundane work. Another Royce rule, similar to the one about not working when the fish were biting. Family was important.

My father moved his car from in front of Lottie's store to the cottage beside the creek. When he got out, instead of shutting the door he turned to me with a question. "Want a visitor for a few days?"

"Of course." Was my father's visit impromptu?

Did he decide to stick around only after Royce gave me the rest of the week off? For whatever reason I was glad because my driven father hadn't had as much time for me growing up as I'd have liked.

I soon learned the visit was, indeed, impromptu. I figured it out because he had no casual clothes, just suits and shiny shoes and ties that probably cost more than my entire wardrobe. Dress for success, he'd always said.

"Any place I can pick up something a little more appropriate?" He waved vaguely at his well clothed body.

"The next town over. Nothing here except one tourist store and a couple businesses for farmers."

He shuddered. "I never thought I'd ever again intentionally be in a tiny, rural town in a farming community for longer than it takes to drive through." He raked a hand through his hair. "Guess I was wrong." He grinned suddenly. "Has your grandfather been waving a magic wand to cast a spell on you?"

"Maybe. I go fly fishing." My father shuddered again and shook his head and I wondered what he'd tell my mother when he went home.

"Do you fish with Royce?" I said that Royce was indeed my fishing buddy and my father nodded as if that told him something. Then he looked around the tiny cottage I so loved that he'd never stay in if there was a better option. "This place looks like you, Susanna."

I agreed and he continued. "Just like the job at the woodworking shop is right for you." My mouth dropped open. "You never did like large corporations." He frowned. "Case in point is your last job though I know there was more than that to your quitting."

It was there again, the look in his face when I'd told him about my job and the exit interview. The look I couldn't read. "But you are glad I left?"

He sighed. "It's probably nothing. Just that something about the whole thing doesn't sound right."

"I was frustrated, that's all. It happens. No big deal."

His face went thoughtful. "People usually sense when things aren't right and that's the vibe I got from you when you described your job. Plus the fact that you weren't promoted and I know you are so over the top with business savvy and skills that you should have been promoted several times during your time there."

"Because you taught me a lot."

He nodded. "But the main thing that bothers me is that exit interview. It's not usual for a low-level employee." Then he waved me to his car because he needed to go clothes shopping.

We spent the rest of that day sightseeing, exploring the area and the several nearby towns and getting him jeans and sweats and sneakers and casual shirts, enough for a few days of visiting and that made my happiness complete. My father bought enough clothes to stay long enough to get a feel for my current life and that was huge considering his discomfort with the rural life.

I wondered what he thought about Southfork and knew he'd only tell me if he approved. Otherwise he'd try his best to hide his dislike and I'd be grateful for that because it meant he loved me in spite of the differences between us.

We returned to Southfork as the sun was dipping towards the west. We pulled up next to the cottage as

Lottie arrived. She waved that she wanted to talk and we waited as she came down the hill, the cottage being at the bottom of a slight hill with the road and the stone bridge that was one of the features of the tiny town at the top.

"Strangers have been asking about you, Susanna." She spoke without preamble as she put her hands on her knees and caught her breath from running across the road and down the hill. "What's going on? Are you wanted for something?" The question was a joke but she wanted to know what was going on.

I was surprised. My father, on the other hand, was concerned. "What are you talking about? Who's been asking?" He used his best upper-level executive voice.

"I didn't know who they were," Lottie said as she got her breath back and straightened up. "But don't worry Susanna, I didn't tell them anything. Neither did anyone else in town. No sir, we don't take kindly to strangers barging in and asking questions about one of our own."

My father's eyes went up. "Susanna's not local." He knew I was now considered local so his statement was a question.

"Yes she is," Lottie said, giving him her best store manager stare. "Ever since our Royce took a liking to her. Hired her. Fed her and gave her half his garden for her own use." She looked him up and down. "We locals circle the wagons when strangers come to town." Letting him know he was a stranger until proven otherwise. "So we clamed up and pretended we didn't know what they were talking about. All of us. Everyone they asked."

She stuck out her lower lip. "They asked for you by

name. Susanna. But they also asked about any new woman in town. We played the part of local rednecks pretty good. They were frustrated, I can tell you that. Thought we were stupid."

She twirled around a couple times. "I was good. They bought it. I could get a job on Broadway, I think. I could have been an actress except then I'd have had to move to New York." She finished with a shudder. "A city. Can you imagine? Ugh."

My father looked towards the stores. "Are those men still here?"

Lottie followed his look. "Must be. That's their car. The black one with the tinted windows." She didn't have to say the car could have been a prop in a gangster movie.

"I think I'll take a look." My father started up the hill towards town proper.

"Not in that suit you won't, "Lottie replied. "You'll stick out like a sore thumb and they'll know something is up."

"You're right." My father grabbed his purchases from the back seat and quickly changed in the cottage's second bedroom. When he came out, though his clothes were new he was closer in appearance to a small town local than before he changed.

As he walked up the hill he scuffed his sneakers and sidetracked through a nearby bush and when he emerged on the road at the top of the hill his clothes no longer looked new and he'd pass for local to someone who didn't know better, especially after he took on a shambling gait that someone from a city might think was rural if they'd watched enough old time westerns.

By the time he reached the first of the few stores in

town, the strangers were ready to leave. They stood beside their shiny, black car and looked around Southfork as if doing so could produce the person they were looking for. Me.

My father shambled along the sidewalk, slowing down as he approached the black car. As he moved to go around them, the strangers stopped him. My heart dropped as one of them grabbed him by the front of his shirt.

My father, without breaking his small-town persona, expertly twisted the hand that held him until it dropped from his shirt. Then he looked the man up and down with a withering stare and then continued on around them without a word. Until another of the strangers spoke. We couldn't hear what he said but could see my father pause and look at him.

There followed a brief conversation during which the strangers formed a circle around my father. An intimidation tactic, but he wasn't bothered in the least. Knowing him, I knew he was returning their stare with one of his own. His best executive type stare and I knew the second he turned it on by the way they backed away. Not much, but enough to know they'd not threaten him again.

Then the conversation ended and they climbed into the back car and left, spitting gravel everywhere with the force of the acceleration. My father returned with a serious expression on his face. He told us what had happened.

"I started around them. I knew they'd not let me go and they didn't. The one guy grabbed my shirt but that didn't last long. Then another guy, probably the leader, spoke. He said, "Sorry. My friend shouldn't have done that." My father's eyes sparked. He enjoyed a good fight. "He said, 'We wanted to ask a question and he's clumsy. That's all.' Then the idiot crossed the sidewalk until he was in front of me. Good blocking technique but I've seen better."

We listened with bated breath as he continued. "We had a little conversation. Pretty much what Lottie said happened when they asked in the stores. They are looking for you, Susanna. Or at least someone named Susanna. Could be a different Susanna, but I suspect it's you they want."

"Did they say why?"

"They pretended to have something for you. Or whomever they are looking for."

"Did you believe them?"

"Of course not." My father considered me thoughtfully. "After what you told Royce and me earlier, I suspect it has to do with that last job you had, the one with the exit interview. Because everything else that's happened to you in the past year was normal. That one thing wasn't."

There was more. I could see it in his eyes. I finally asked, "What aren't you telling us?"

He folded his arms in front of his chest and was silent for a long time. When he spoke his words were quiet. Too quiet. "Those goons reminded me of a couple guys I met in a job I once had. We had a few meetings. I was glad when I didn't work with them any longer. I later learned they were members of organized crime."

We were silent for a long time. Finally my father quietly said, "When my visit here is done and I go home, I think I'll make a few inquiries."

Chapter 8

"I don't have any enemies. There's no reason for you to ask around."

My father rocked back on his heels. "You're probably right but I think I will anyway." He shrugged and didn't fool me one bit. "Might as well. Something to do when I'm bored."

Then he changed the subject. "What say we see what your friend Royce is doing for dinner. Maybe get together for the evening." He looked around at the countryside with the eyes of a city person. "And see if there's anything to do in Southfork." He sighed. "Anything at all."

Royce offered to cook a fish dinner. My father looked like he'd puke. "I'd rather not."

"You don't like fish?"

My father colored slightly. "My father – Susanna's grandfather – loved to fish so I grew up eating fish dinners. Lots of them." We were in Royce's kitchen and my father looked around as if hoping something would pop up. Steaks. Hamburgers. Anything but fish. "Is there a pizza place nearby? I'll pay."

"No pizza place. We eat at home in Southfork."

We had pork chops that my father and Royce ate with gusto and I enjoyed at a slower pace because, after all, it was dinner instead of a marathon eating contest. I didn't remember my father eating with such enjoyment when I was a kid but I reasoned that he was now in the country and was possibly reverting back to his childhood on my grandparents' farm. Farmers tend to have healthy appetites.

After dinner my father suggested we check out the creek he'd heard rushing past my rented cottage but hadn't yet seen. So we dragged chairs and carried pop and cookies to the shore and spent the evening watching water move from one place to another around and over a bunch of rocks before heading to parts unknown.

The sound of the river was such that there was little conversation. I'd have missed his question to Royce except I turned away from the mesmerizing creek in time to see him lean close and speak. So I listened without appearing to because he wasn't including me in whatever he was about to say.

He reminded Royce of his interaction with the strangers in town. Then he told him about his plan to make some inquiries after leaving Southfork. Then he said something more. "I'm concerned about Susanna."

"Sounds like you might have good reason to be."

"I'll be gone. She'll be here. This tiny cottage is not safe."

Royce was still for a moment. Then he spoke. "I'll keep an eye on her."

"I was hoping you'd say that."

"She works for me and does her classes in the office so we're together most of the time anyway." He cocked his head in thought. "If strangers come to Southfork everyone in town will know it just as they did today. Especially if it's that same black car. It's pretty obvious with tinted windows and everything. It's a city car." He stuck his legs out and examined the sturdy leather boots he favored because they were right for working in his shop. "Don't worry about a thing. We'll keep her safe."

My father sighed. "I hope never to live in a small town again but they have features I'm grateful for and keeping tabs on strangers and protecting their own are two of the best." He finished with, "I'm glad Susanna is here and I'm glad she works for you, Royce."

Then he turned back to the creek and the evening proceeded as if there'd been no discussion between the two of them and later when Royce went home and my father and I went into the cottage he said nothing to me and I didn't mention that I'd overheard anything.

The next few days stretched out in lazy warmth. My father had no desire to fly fish though he'd done it as a boy but he encouraged me to do it with him watching from a chair on the bank while reading one of the books he always brought to business meetings because it gave him something to do in motels. I put my catches in the freezer and made sure we had no fish meals at all. Not even seafood.

The fourth day, he suggested I go to work. "Making furniture sounds interesting. Maybe I can watch while you do whatever it is you do." So we trudged across the street and Royce said the books could use a little tender loving care and that, since I'd fallen a little behind in my online classes, I maybe should catch up while I was there.

My father said he'd watch Royce make furniture while I kept the door closed between the shop and the office to keep sawdust out of the computers. I watched them both through the windows that separated the shop from the office. After a while my father left. He went outside. I figured he'd visit Lottie in her store and buy something for my mother so I turned back to my laptop when the door from the outside opened a second time and I looked to see what he'd forgotten.

It wasn't my father. It was the strangers who'd asked about me earlier. The ones I thought had left town. I took one look at them and froze. They were well dressed. Clean. Neat. Polite. And something about the way they just stood there quietly frightened me so much it was all I could do to shut off the computer and close it and wait for whatever was about to happen.

Royce, on the other hand, was as laid back and casual as ever. If he had any thoughts about them at all, it didn't show. He smiled and shook their hands and acted as if they were customers come to ask about a furniture order even though he'd never had a customer come to his shop before. His eyes flicked to me and away so quickly that none of the men noticed.

They talked. With the door closed I couldn't hear what they said. I opened my computer again so I it would look like I was working. I had to do something, I couldn't just sit there and wait for – whatever. And when Royce and the men headed towards the office, I managed to take a deep breath and look like I was working and not concerned about anything at all. I hoped I gave that impression. I was afraid I didn't.

Royce opened the door. "Honey, these men are looking for a newcomer in town. A woman." He blinked, then came close and wrapped an arm around me casually. "Seen anyone, sweetheart? I haven't but it occurred to me that maybe you have." His arm squeezed me. Hard. As in sending a message for me to play along.

"I haven't seen anyone," I said, managing to speak over the lump in my throat. Royce squeezed me harder, the gesture telling me I was doing great and to keep it up.

"I guess we can't help you," he said to the men as his arm slid lower until it reached my waist. Then he pulled me close until we were so tight I could feel him breathe "And neither did I see anyone, though I tend not to notice other women." He looked at the men. "Marriage is such a great thing. Isn't it?" And he squeezed me. Again.

He was pretending I was his wife and hadn't used my name because they were looking for someone named Susanna. He smiled down at me and I tried to smile back. I managed a sickly half smile and leaned against him because right then I needed something solid before my legs gave out and I fell. He pulled me in front of him and wrapped his other arm around me, keeping me upright. He knew what I was feeling and was supporting me.

The men watched without any emotion. Then the leader frowned and said something under his breath to the others and they turned to go. "We'll find her eventually. It's just a matter of time."

Royce spoke without letting up on me. "Maybe you're looking in the wrong place. There are a number of small towns in the area. The woman you seek could be in any of them."

The leader didn't follow his men out of the office. Instead he looked at the computers on the desk. "This is where the internet address led us." He gave the office a thorough inspection. "She's in Southfork." He moved after his men. "We'll find her, no doubt of that." He brushed his hands together to rid himself of the sawdust he'd gathered during his brief time in the shop. "And we'll be able to give her the news we've been tasked with telling her."

"What news is that?" Royce asked politely.

"It's for her to hear and her only," he said as he turned to make his way back through the shop to the outside world. "If you see her, call me." He handed Royce a business card. "Believe me, it'll be in her best interest."

As the door closed behind him Royce muttered in my ear. "If he thinks I'll give you up because he's pretending to have some great news, then he's dumber than he looks. And he looks pretty dumb." He kept his arms wrapped around me until I got my feet back under me and was able to stand on my own.

Chapter 9

Royce let go of me and I managed to stand unaided. "Sorry about the marriage bit. Glad you figured out what I was doing and played along." He went back into the shop and shook himself. Sawdust flew everywhere and then, relatively free of the dust that could harm computers, he returned to the office.

"Your father is concerned about you. He doesn't trust those guys and I don't trust them either – we are in complete agreement -- and you being my wife was the first thing I thought to say when they came looking for you."

"Thank you." It was all I could say. All I could manage. I sank to the chair. "It has to be a mistake. All of it."

"Didn't seem like a mistake to me. Why do you think that?"

"Because there's no reason for anyone to want me. Not to hurt me or to tell me I just inherited a million dollars, which is what they are trying to make you think so you'd give me up."

"I'd never do that."

"I know. But the thing is, none of this makes sense. I'm just me and I'm in Southfork to take a few classes and go fishing. Nothing serious. So it's a mistake. It's got to be."

"What did you do at your last job?"

"Clerk stuff. Occasional bookkeeping but not much. Nothing important enough to justify someone coming after me." I closed my laptop because I'd not be able to do anything more. I was too shook up. "That's why I'm sure it's a case of mistaken identity."

"It doesn't matter why. I think your father is right. Something is going on. You should be extra alert."

"I'm the wrong woman. They'll figure that out and forget about me."

Just then the door to the shop opened once more. Both Royce and I jumped because it could be them returning. But it was my father, carrying a largish paper bag. So I'd been right and he had a gift for my mother.

He came straight to the office and looked from Royce to me. "What happened?" Because it was clear something had. Royce explained and my father breathed sharply. "Thank you, Royce." He hugged me. "Be careful, Susanna."

I promised because those men in black were scary and I didn't want to have to deal with them again. I didn't like the feeling they gave me. That I had a target on my back. Not that they were actually evil because that wouldn't make sense. After all, there was no reason criminals would have anything to do with an average, normal person like me.

My father stuck around for the next three days. I was pretty sure he'd planned on leaving before then because he always bought my mother a gift on his last day wherever he was. But when men came looking for me he changed his mind and stayed until they were gone for sure.

In those three days we both got to know the entire town because my father needed something to do. Keeping active was part of his hyperactive, over-the-top CEO persona.

We took walks. On one such walk we checked out the feed store. We learned the owner's name was George and that he'd carved out a space in his store for a circle of comfortable chairs around a table that held a huge coffee container and a few boxes of sweet rolls, compliments of one or another of the people around the table because there was no bakery in town.

"It's the town center," my father informed me when we were once more outside after having met most of the nearby farmers who were having coffee and rolls and discussing the weather. "The place where everyone gathers to talk and be social. Every small town has one. Usually it's a café but Southfork isn't big enough to support a restaurant so the feed store is it."

He had a faraway look in his eyes. "Reminds me of my childhood." But he finished with, "I'm glad I don't live here." He rumpled my hair and kissed the top of my head. "Though you seem to fit in quite well."

We also met the owner of the farm implement store, Lyle, an elderly man with a few gray hairs who wanted to show off the latest and largest farm equipment available anywhere except we wouldn't appreciate them because we knew nothing about farming so I figured he'd realize that soon and stop talking. That is, *I* didn't know anything.

My father, on the other hand, knew enough from his farm childhood to listen intelligently as Lyle talked his arm off, nodding and pretending to be interested.

Again, when we left, my father simply said it was a farming community. But his eyes said he remembered another such community with fondness even though he'd left as soon as he finished high school.

Then he repeated what he'd said earlier. "I think your grandfather waved a magic wand and created some kind of spell that drew you to this town that he'd describe as a little piece of Heaven." He shook his head and gazed around at the few buildings and fewer people that made up Southfork. And the dog and two cats wandering along the main street.

Then he grinned. "I can't think of a single other way you ended up here so it had to be a magic spell. But, Susanna, you look happy and that's all that matters." Then he added, "That is, you're happy when those nut cases in the black car aren't around with their nasty looks and intrusive questions."

The next day, after stopping by the woodworking shop to say goodbye, he left. When he was gone I mentioned to Royce that the two of them had talked for quite a while, standing beside my father's car with the door open before my father got in. "Of course," was Royce's response. "We had to get each other's contact information. And decide on a strategy. And so on."

"What are you talking about? Why do you need a strategy? For what?"

He looked at me as if I was a six-year-old child who didn't know what the grownups were doing. "We were discussing your safety."

"Huh!" I didn't know whether to be grateful or insulted. "I don't need protection. I told you I'm the wrong woman so I'll never see those men again."

"I hope you are right." But Royce's expression said

he'd continue to act as if I was in danger.

"You and my father are going to talk about me whether I agree or not and figure things to do to keep me safe whether I need protection or not. Aren't you?"

"Yes we are until we are sure there's no longer a reason to do so." His eyes softened. "And there's nothing you can do about it so you might as well accept it."

I opened my laptop with an irritated snap and stared at the days' bookkeeping and somehow managed to actually know what I was looking at as I didn't reply because what can you say to something like that? When I finished the bookkeeping I got caught up with my online classes. I glowered at the laptop the whole time. But by quitting time I'd come to accept that for the near future I'd be watched and protected and, though I didn't want to admit it, I felt better because of it.

As the days passed I realized my father's visit had changed things for me in more ways than dealing with scary men. I now joined Royce when he meandered over to the feed store for coffee and donuts because I'd been there with my father and now it felt comfortable. After the first time, the farmers brought out another chair for me and told Royce to make sure I came.

After all, they said, even though I'd grown up in cities because my father worked for large corporations, my roots were in small town America and they honored that fact with a chair just for me, a coffee cup with my name on it in black magic marker and a daily donut. Or two. Or three.

Once I figured out how things worked I took my turn providing the morning baked goods. I was glad that as a child I'd helped my mother bake so when my father came home tired and cross we could present him with yummy desserts and hot chocolate. Soon he'd be smiling. Every. Single. Time. Now that childhood habit came in handy.

Royce liked baked treats. "I can cook but I can't bake." He finished still another cinnamon roll with frosting. His third. "Together we make a good team. I cook and you bake." He rubbed his stomach. "Though such a partnership could lead to an increase in untold numbers of pounds in a short time so maybe sticking to furniture is a better use of my time."

He rose. "Speaking of which, we should get to work." I liked the sound of that 'we' and followed him to the shop that was becoming one of my favorite places in Southfork, along with the creek, the stone bridge, the fields that now were covered with late spring flowers, Lottie's tourist store and – and – everything. The whole town. The entire area.

When we reached the shop I stopped short of the door. Royce almost plowed into me. "What's wrong?"

"Something moved." I sounded afraid even to myself.

"Who? What? Where?" He looked about. "Are they back? The men in black?" Just like that he was on alert, seeming to grow inches and turn into granite as his eyes sparked darkly dangerous. "I'll deal with them."

"It's too small to be people." I held my arms about a foot apart to show him the size of the mystery presence while examining the space between the door and me, unwilling to cross it because I was sure I'd seen something move. Royce returned to his usual laid-back mode even as I took a step back and stared some more, this time intently. But I saw nothing.

Royce stepped around me. "Are you afraid?" He didn't laugh but struggled to keep a straight face. "Because I don't see anything to be afraid of."

"Yep. Terrified." I took another step backwards. "I know I saw something. I know I did. It wasn't imaginary."

"I'll check it out." He moved forward a bit more, still trying unsuccessfully not to laugh. "Don't worry. I promise to protect you from any stray cats or rabbits that stopped by for a visit." Because that was the approximate size of the mystery intruder.

I didn't care. I wasn't about to venture forth without knowing what lay in wait in the tall grass beside the door.

As Royce drew close to the shop door, whatever it was moved again. This time he saw it too and hesitated before moving closer. Then it moved again, distancing itself from Royce. He stopped and waited.

We both watched as the movement in the grass turned into a small, black and white puppy. It was skinny and dirty and barely had enough strength to walk the few steps to Royce, who gathered it in his arms and hugged it gently.

"Hi, little one," he said softly as he turned to show me what had scared me so thoroughly. Those brown-gold eyes that changed from one shade to another depending on his mood showed his concern for the small, exhausted animal.

"We have to take care of him." I went close and stroked the tiny, disgustingly dirty animal.

Royce examined the puppy's underbelly. "Not 'him.' It's a 'her'."

"She needs help."

"And food. And a bath."

I examined the man before me holding the small creature so carefully. "So are we going to get any work done or not?"

"Not until this little girl is okay." The tiny thing cuddled closer to Royce's chest and I was glad for his belief that some things were more important than regular work hours. "Food first, and water. Then a bath. Then a visit with the vet." He sighed. "I can work through the night." He grinned suddenly. "It won't be the first time, though usually it's because the fish were biting and I just kept fishing until the sun went down."

Puppy things took up the rest of the day. When the sun finally went down there was a small, clean black and white puppy curled on a few old towels in Royce's kitchen with two adults watching it sleep as if it was the most fascinating thing ever.

"She's mine," I said without thinking. The vet had checked everywhere and everyone he knew without finding an owner. I'd never had a pet and she drew me.

"What about when you leave Southfork?"

The notion of leaving was sudden and jarring. "I don't know."

"Tell you what. She's yours while you are here but, if when you leave you can't have a dog where you go, then I'll take her."

"You don't have a dog." I'd noticed that the first time I was in his house because he seemed like the kind of guy to have one.

"I did until recently. Ruffalo had a long life but dogs don't live as long as people."

"So you're okay with Cleo when I leave?"

"Cleo? She already has a name?"

"After Cleopatra. Queen of the Nile. This isn't the Nile, it's the south branch of the Southfork River but the concept is the same."

"She's on the small side to be a queen but she'll grow into her name." He sighed and checked the calendar. "And it'll be doubly busy for the next week or so because I must occasionally actually get some work done in the shop but Cleo needs to be acclimated to her new home so you're going to have to do it." He rubbed the back of his neck. "You know how many orders we have."

"You aren't behind."

"I will be soon if I don't get busy." His look met mine. "Good thing I now have an employee who isn't afraid of scary men in black but goes ballistic when one small puppy sneaks through the grass."

"It could have been something dangerous."

"Like a bunny rabbit?"

He picked up Cleo who was still sleeping. He wrapped her in the towels and handed her to me. "Go home, Susanna. Teach her where she lives. She's welcome to stay with me any time but if you want her to be your puppy then she must get used to you and your home."

As I started to leave, Royce stopped me, using a foot to block me from opening the door. Then, as before, he simply leaned down and kissed me. And Cleo. Then he opened the door and waved us off. It took the entire few minute walk from his place to my cottage for my insides to settle back to normal.

It had been a standard Royce kiss. No escalation, no increase in intensity. More than friendly but less than sexual. My reaction, however, had definitely felt different. I was going beyond friendship. Way beyond. And I knew with bone deep certainty that I'd be drawn deeper into the Royce Adamson milieu with each successive kiss.

It was a scary thought because surely Royce Adamson kissed a lot. It was his thing. Undoubtedly he kissed moms, grandmas, puppies, and me though so far I'd only become aware of Cleo and me. But in spite of knowing he kissed everyone, with all the kissing of me how would I feel by the time the summer ended? Would I be able to walk? Eat? Speak? Function at all? I sincerely doubted it.

Chapter 10

Cleo loved her new home. The next morning she explored every nook and cranny of the small cottage with her tail wagging and excitement in every pore. Royce showed up before breakfast to tell me I could bring her to the woodworking shop. That I should bring her so she wouldn't feel abandoned. He insisted he'd enjoy having her around as long as I kept her in the office where she wouldn't be in danger around the machinery or get covered with sawdust that would be deposited later all over the cottage.

That evening, after work, Royce invited Cleo and me to dinner at his place. "So she'll get used to my house. I want her to visit often." In less time than I'd have thought possible the small puppy was at home in all three places. Cottage, workshop and Royce's home. But the cottage beside the creek was her favorite. As it was mine.

Royce got caught up on furniture orders. "I hear the trout are hitting." He looked around the shop with a satisfied expression that said he knew how to organize his life without schedules, thank you very much, and he was dancing with eagerness to get back in the creek with a fly rod and creel.

He'd been working late into the night so he could go fishing when the trout started hitting again. He didn't believe in schedules but he did believe in hard work.

So the next morning with the shop empty, I slept in. When I was finally up and functional and Cleo had been fed and walked in the field behind the cottage that she'd chosen as her personal bathroom, I decided that after breakfast she and I would check out the creek because that was where we'd find Royce.

Maybe I'd be able to creep up on him unnoticed. Maybe the sun would shine on him as it had that first day and would once again turn him into a Greek god. Or at least a very good-looking fly fisherman. And maybe we'd get a shore lunch out of the deal. I explained it all to Cleo as we ate breakfast and she listened intently and wagged her tail in agreement.

We'd dawdled over breakfast and also in the fields that were sweet with summer wildflowers so we were still at the cottage when a car pulled up. A black car with tinted windows. I froze. I was alone except for Cleo, and terrified.

Three men got out. I couldn't tell if they were the same men who'd visited the woodworking shop. If not, they were clones of those men and not in a nice way. An air of menace hovered over them as I put on the bravest front I could manage after giving myself a stern lecture about thinking the worst when it probably wasn't indicated. Then I went outside and managed to ask what they wanted.

"We're looking for Susanna Brown. We were told she's renting this cottage." They looked me up and down. Their eyes narrowed because they recognized me from the woodworking shop. "Are you Susanna?"

"I'm Susanna Adamson." As Royce would have told the last contingent of nasty men in black hoodies if they'd asked.

"Then what are you doing here? This isn't your home." They dared me to come up with an explanation.

I thought fast. "It's a rental cottage. Perhaps the Susanna you are looking for rented it earlier. If so, she's gone now. I'm cleaning it between rentals because Mrs. Sanders is elderly and not up to doing it herself." I held my breath and hoped they'd believe me.

They didn't, not even close, but there was no way for them to prove I was lying. I shut the door firmly so they couldn't see my things carelessly strewn about inside or my clothes in the closet with the doors still open from when I'd gotten dressed.

I could see them thinking. Figuring what to ask next that would give them the information they sought without threatening me. Because, if I was telling the truth, threats could backfire and bring the law down on them. They didn't want that. I could see it in their expressions.

One of them, probably the leader, smiled without the smile reaching his eyes. "So we missed her. Susanna Brown has come and gone." He smiled wider, still without a glimmer of humor. "But that creates a problem for us. Perhaps you can help."

I went on alert. The leader spoke in what was meant to be a casual voice and wasn't casual all. "Susanna Brown worked for a company similar to the one we represent. We were hoping to speak with her." He looked at the others and they nodded imperceptibly that they'd back up whatever he was about to say. "To get her expertise and pay her well for it."

He looked around. He didn't care about the cottage or the scenery. The gesture was merely to give himself time to think what to say next. "This is a nice place. Pretty." When I said nothing, he elaborated. "It's rural and that means property is cheap compared to other places."

"I suppose so." I demurred and picked Cleo up and held her close. Her small, warm body calmed me and slowed my too rapid heartbeat as I wished Royce was there because he'd be better than me at playing these men's game, whatever it was.

The leader continued. "We were hoping for Susanna Brown's insights. Not only for the business we hope to start in Southfork, but to the area itself. If she thinks our idea will work. If the infrastructure potential is acceptable. All kinds of things."

I wanted them gone. But they stood like statues, still and threatening. So I simply waited for their next move. The leader looked around for a second time, seeming to see the cottage for the first time as he had an idea. "You said this is a rental?"

I nodded and he continued. "I wonder if we could rent it for a while? A week or so? Since Susanna Brown isn't here to talk with, it would be a useful way for us to get a feel for the town. To talk to people. To find out if they'd like another business here. You know, jobs for local people and all that. A good thing for the town."

He waited for me to say something. To argue or to agree. Anything. But my tongue was stuck to the roof of my mouth and I struggled to speak because their threat was clear.

They weren't going away. They'd use whatever

excuse they could come up with to stick around and would remain until they'd got what they wanted.

I cleared my throat and spoke. "Too bad the cottage is rented for the entire summer." Would that make them leave?

That evil smile grew wider. "Yes, that's too bad." He leered. "What other places are for rent in Southfork?" He examined me, no longer trying to be polite because scaring me would be more productive and his threatening manner without saying anything specific would work just fine. And it did. I was terrified and he knew it.

"I don't know of any other place to rent. It's a small town. Not even a tourist town. Just a dot on the map. A crossroads."

He folded his arms and leaned against the porch in a gesture that could be casual or a deliberate threat. I knew which it was and shrank. "Well then, there's nothing more for us to do here." He looked at the other men in black hoodies and they responded by preparing to leave while checking me out from top to bottom in a way that sent shivers through me. "We'll find a place to stay in one of the nearby towns, I'm sure." He gave a half salute that didn't fool me at all. "See you around, Susanna." With an emphasis on my name so I'd know that he didn't for a second believe I was Susanna Adamson. He knew better. I was Susanna Brown, the woman he was looking for and, in time, he'd prove it and come for me.

They he levered himself off the porch and the three men returned to that black car with tinted windows and in the space of less than a minute they were gone and I sank to the porch steps, still holding Cleo tightly because I needed her small, warm body against mine and against the threat I'd barely managed to avoid.

I dropped Cleo to the ground and headed for the creek, hoping Royce would be there. As soon as I stepped into the shade of the trees arching over the creek I felt better and took several deep breaths and let the peace of the area settle over me.

Cleo, of course, ran everywhere and chased a frog into the creek but wasn't brave enough to follow it into the water so she sat on the shore and yipped softly in frustration. The normal action calmed me still more until I was able to look for Royce.

Chapter 11

Royce was there, in the same spot in the creek where he'd been that first day and, like that day, dappled sun shone through the trees and turned him into a work of art, a dance of light and shadow with the line from his rod flashing back and forth in a rhythm as old as time. And just as reassuring. Royce was nearby, the men in the black hoodies were gone and the world was safe once more.

Unlike that first day, though, this time he sensed my presence. He turned, nodded to me and after a pause while his fly rested on the surface of the water, he reeled it in, stuck the hook in the cork handle of his rod, and climbed out of the creek to stand beside me.

"What's wrong and don't try to say nothing because something clearly is bothering you and it's bad." He leaned his rod against a tree trunk after making sure the tip wouldn't get caught in the branches, then came close and gathered me in his arms. He murmured softly, his lips brushing my ear. "Whatever it is, it's okay now." Yes it was okay because he was there and I soaked up the safety of his presence.

"They were back."

He drew in his breath quickly and hard and put me

away from him. "Did they do anything? Did they hurt you?"

"They came to the cottage. I told them Susanna Brown has left but they knew better. They know I'm her but they can't prove it."

"This is getting serious." He pulled me back and wrapped his arms around me. It was an instinctive move, the protective male caring for the nearest fragile female and I was fine with it. "You're moving in with me."

"No I'm not." I struggled against his arms, knowing as I did so that it was what I wanted because it would be safe. But I refused to be a coward, no matter that I felt like one at the moment. I wouldn't let the men in black hoodies scare me out of my lovely cottage. I would find bravery somewhere in me no matter how deep I had to dig. "There's a line they won't cross. I saw it during their visit. They don't want to do anything illegal so all they can do is talk. That means I'll be fine."

He frowned. "For now. But what about later if talking doesn't get them what they want? What about then? What if they return and are out for blood?"

"If that happens I'll move in with you. But it won't. Their little threats won't work with me and though no precise words were spoken, they got that message. They know I'm not a frightened little woman." Royce didn't like it but I was steadfast in my determination and nothing he could say would change my mind. "So you can continue fishing. It's a good day for it."

"Are you kidding? You think I can stand in the creek and cast a line knowing nasty men are after you?

If you think I can do that, then you don't know me." And he proceeded to gather his fishing gear. "Besides, I caught enough for lunch if we add a few veggies from the garden. So if you and Cleo will follow me we can head to my place and enjoy the fruits of my labors." He considered his words. "And yours because we can add radishes from your half of the garden and maybe some lettuce from mine. We can have a farm meal."

"Like at my grandfather's after we'd fished in the stream that ran along his property and picked tomatoes on the way back."

It was a truly nice lunch. Probably no different than what I'd have had in any restaurant in the city but it seemed better. More delicious. Definitely more leisurely because Royce wouldn't have it any other way. He heaped praise on the radishes in the salad as if the rest of it, the part he'd grown, wasn't worthy of mention. I'd read radishes were easy to grow but appreciated his words.

Maybe if I returned to the city I'd look for a place with a garden. And why was that sudden thought depressing? I chose not to explore why returning to my former life sent me into a depression because I was afraid if I looked too deeply I'd find Southfork growing on me.

Maybe not the town itself, perhaps it was the inhabitants I found so appealing. Or, to be honest, one inhabitant in particular who was sitting across the table from me eating with the gusto outdoor types seemed to specialize in.

After lunch Royce decided he needed fertilizer for the garden. "It's looking a bit jaded."

"How can you tell?" My question led to a second

visit to the garden so he could point out slightly droopy leaves. "Not from lack of rain because this is turning out to be a rainy summer so it's got to be a lack of nutrients."

"And the feed store will know what we need?"

"It's their business to know stuff like that."

"Should I leave Cleo at your place?"

"It's a country store. She'll be welcome but it might be smart to carry her so she doesn't disappear into some corner and scarf down food that might not be good for her." So I wrapped Cleo in my sweater and the three of us crossed the street to the feed store.

When Royce described the droopy leaves, George knew exactly what we needed. As he handed Royce a bag of fertilizer, he turned to me. "You're a popular woman."

"In what way?" I expected him to say something about my chair at the coffee table, or the cup with my name on it. I didn't expect him to mention the men in black hoodies.

"Three guys were here a while ago asking about you." He acted a bit confused. "That is, I think they were asking about you. They wanted to know about someone named Susanna but when they described you they thought you were Royce's wife."

He rang up the charges and Royce paid automatically but I could see his back muscles tighten as George continued. "The thing is they described you perfectly." His gaze swept over me to make sure I fit the description the men had given. "And I don't believe there are two Suzannas in town."

"Must have been a case of mistaken identity even if they did describe her. There are lots of smallish women with long, light brown hair," Royce said in a voice so unnatural that George's eyes slit and swept Royce much harder than when they'd looked me over.

George backed up a bit and took in both of us together in a steady but still confused gaze. "I told them you aren't married, Royce." He'd backed up to better see how his comment affected us and didn't like the sudden quiet that settled over us. "Was that the right thing to say?" He finished with, "They weren't nice guys, that much was evident. Thugs of some kind."

He waited for an answer and finally Royce said, "Sure. They are gone by now, whomever they were, so it doesn't matter what you said." George wasn't placated so he added, "They stopped by the shop a while back and Susanna was there because she's working for me now."

He shrugged a little too elaborately. "Guess they made some assumptions and decided we were husband and wife." George wasn't fooled by Royce's little speech. He knew there was more to what was going on than Royce was willing to say but he remained silent and simply handed Royce his bag of fertilizer.

He took it and grabbed my hand and led me out of the feed store but I felt George's look until the door slammed behind us. His concern was palpable.

"We should head for the workshop and deal with new orders." Some had trickled in as was usual in Royce's business. The paperwork for me to figure out and the actual furniture for Royce to make.

Neither of us spoke as we trudged the short distance. I stroked Cleo in my arms so hard she should have lost her fur and sparks emanated from Royce's eyes that were now almost black with anger.

Two days later, we learned there was a takeaway from our conversation with George. We were at the tourist store where I'd gone to buy a sweatshirt because everything I had was dirty. Royce let me do laundry at his place because the cottage lacked a washer and dryer, something the ad for it had failed to mention. I usually waited till everything was dirty to bring it over and do it all at once. A mistake, I'd learned, when enough of a breeze sprang up for me to look for something warm to put over my thin blouse and couldn't find anything that was clean.

Royce helped me pick out a fluffy pink sweatshirt with a picture of the stone bridge on it. According to Lottie it was a favorite with the occasional tourist who meandered into Southfork. Then she said, "I hear you and Royce are an item."

"Huh?" I stopped in the act of reaching for my purchase with one hand while holding Cleo with the other. "What are you talking about?"

"It's all over town. The two of you are a couple, no question about it. You do everything together. You work together. Fish together. Eat together. Go everywhere together. And so on." She smiled broadly. "You might as well be joined at the hip."

She sighed mightily. "It's about time Royce got serious about someone. It's hard to connect with anyone in a place this small so it's a blessing you came along, Susanna. You are definitely the right woman in the right place at the right time."

"There's nothing between us." I turned red and held Cleo and the bag containing the sweatshirt as buffers between me and the gossip Lottie accepted as truth as I avoided looking at Royce and was sure he was avoiding me.

"So you say." Lottie's grin was conspiratorial. "But we folks in Southfork know better. Because we know Royce and now we know you." She waved at me vaguely. "Look at you. Then look at Royce. You two are made for each other. You even share a puppy." She scratched Cleo behind the ears and happily escorted us to the door. "It's just a matter of time, dear."

She shooed us along the sidewalk with the air of someone who couldn't wait to pass on the news that she'd talked with the object of Royce's affections in person and could report with certainty that there'd soon be wedding bells ringing in Southfork.

In the workshop, wearing a bright pink sweatshirt with Cleo settled happily in a corner on the old towels Royce had provided, I sought him out. "Everyone in town thinks we are engaged."

He blinked but there was no other reaction to my words. "Of course."

"Is that all you can say?"

"It's a small town and I had the bad judgement to tell those guys we were married. The result is the town has us engaged, married, and, for all I know, with a kid on the way and it'll all happen before the snow flies."

"That's ridiculous."

"It's not ridiculous. It's small-town America in action." He put down the board he'd been ready to cut on the huge table saw that took up a fair amount of space in the shop. "It's the gossip mill. Small town America's way of making sure future generations come into existence."

"What do we do about it?"

"Nothing we can do except ignore it. Or enjoy it."

He set the board aside and let his eyes light up and turn gold. Did he stop working because the saw was dangerous and he'd best not use it while he was adjusting to the news that he was the subject of town gossip? Or was it merely because the board hadn't been measured correctly?

"I do plan on getting married someday." He considered what he'd said. "That is, I hope to get married. But you know how it is. Not many eligible females in Southfork. Lottie was right about that." He thought a moment. "In fact there aren't *any* eligible females in town. Except you."

"And I'm temporary."

"Plus you might not be the marrying kind."

"I am the marrying kind." I spoke without thinking and my words were a bit huffy. Then I retracted them. "I want to get married eventually. Like you do. When I meet the right guy. If I meet him. Then and only then will it happen."

"That's a high bar to meet but it's the same bar I'm dealing with. So I understand where you're coming from." He took the board once more and pulled out his tape measure with a scowl. "We both might be single forever."

"How depressing."

"Yep."

He put the board aside as if it was poison and stuffed his tape measure back in his pocket as we stared at one another wordlessly. Then he said, "Lack of eligible life partners is a depressing topic and I'm tired of thinking depressing thoughts. What about you? Are you up for doing something creative that'll put a smile on your face? And on mine?"

"What are you thinking?"

"I don't know. Grab Cleo and let's go outside and look for happiness. Or sunshine. Or maybe plant something in the garden now that we have fertilizer because growing things will make us happy." He took my elbow and steered me towards the office and Cleo. "Let's do something to take our minds off our miserable matrimonial prospects."

Chapter 12

We spent a small amount of time in the garden but it didn't make us smile enough. Too much work. "What say we walk along the creek? It's pretty and you've never seen it beyond the stretch near your cottage." Royce added, "We can take Cleo. She'll like it."

So we sauntered across the road and headed for the creek that seemed to be calling us with a low murmur that surely said something though I couldn't quite make it out. That the day was beautiful even without being in love? That I should just enjoy nature and not worry about romance? Somehow, neither felt right. They weren't speaking to what I was thinking. Maybe it was just water rippling over rocks.

Chloe ran one way and another, loving every minute of her exploration and putting more miles on than we could count as we moved slowly along the creek bank. Once I stumbled and Royce caught me before I fell and when I righted myself our hands stayed together and we continued on down the creek but slower. One step at a time. And somehow the slowness itself was intimate in a way walking normally hadn't been.

"We should go fishing tomorrow," Royce said out

of nowhere as we reached an opening in the trees and stopped to let the sun warm us before continuing on. "Better than working." Of course the consummate fisherman said that.

"Sounds good," I answered. "What about Cleo?"

"Maybe Lottie can watch her. I hate to let her run around while we are fishing. She might chase after the lines and get caught by a hook."

"Think the trout will be biting?"

"I'm sure of it." Unsaid was that it didn't matter if we caught anything or not. It would be a good day and after our depressing discussion of our single futures, anything positive would be valuable.

Lottie was fine with Cleo, saying she'd be a big help. "She'll keep me company if it's a slow day and will keep kids happy if I'm busy with their parents."

So the next day Royce and I spent several hours standing in the creek in waders. I spent more time watching him than fishing. The man was gorgeous. There was no other way to describe him when he was in his element, thigh deep in rushing water with a pole in his hands and that incredible dappled sun turning him into light and shadow.

Of course, the creek itself was gorgeous. Full summer had arrived and the leaves overhead were now deep green and thick and the fields of wildflowers were no longer the yellow and pink of spring. Instead they wore the deeper colors of summer and were harder to find nestled in the thick, green grass that would eventually be cut for hay.

What would the fields be like when autumn came? I pictured the purples and oranges of fall and wondered if I'd see them. When should I start looking for another job if I left Southfork? When should I write up a new resume and how many copies should I make? How long would it take to find my next job? What would it be? Where would I live?

Something tugged on my line. I was so deep in thought I'd forgotten what I was doing and it got away. Royce noticed. Of course he did and tipped his head in my direction to ask what was going on. I waved that all was good and he returned to his line and soon dropped another trout into his creel. Mine was empty. As usual.

I couldn't keep my mind on fishing, which wasn't normal for me. My grandfather had taught me about fishing. It was important and required constant alertness even during the slow times when it seemed nothing was happening because those were the times I'd be most likely to get a bite and if I wasn't paying attention I'd not bring dinner home.

But that day I couldn't concentrate. Instead of trout I thought about Royce. And winter. And Southfork. I might be there during autumn but winter was out of the question because my quaint cottage wasn't winterized. The pipes would freeze and so would I because the walls weren't insulated well enough to keep the inside warm.

As I stood in that rushing water I realized I wanted to see winter in Southfork. I wanted to walk with Royce through new snow and kick it until it blew everywhere. I wanted to help decorate the town for Christmas and perhaps ride a sleigh behind a team of horses. Surely someone in the area had horses and a sleigh and gave rides to the neighbors. They must because it was a small-town thing.

"Hey." I was startled. "You were dreaming and

there's a fish on your line and you don't even know it." Royce gently took my pole and brought in the nicest trout of the day. And he put it in his creel instead of mine, waiting to see if I'd argue that it belonged to me and should be in my creel. But I didn't, I just let him gather my pole and line and then I followed him to shore, letting him hand me up the very bank that I'd fallen from that first day in Southfork.

We walked in comfortable silence to the cottage where I put my fishing things away. Then, without saying a word we picked up Cleo from Lottie and headed for his house and dinner because that was what we always did after a day spent fishing.

"You're thoughtful," Royce said quietly after dinner as we adjourned to his back yard and deck chairs with comfortable cushions and Cleo ran around the yard, glad to be active after a day in Lottie's store. "Anything you care to share with me?"

"I don't want to leave Southfork. Ever." I didn't know I was going to say it until the words were out. I didn't know I'd been sure of my feelings until I heard myself say them. But after they were said, I knew they were true and were what I wanted. "Not that there's any way I can stay permanently."

"Why not?" He was his usual Royce self. Laid back and easy going but this time he was more gentle than usual. Because he heard my wishful thinking? "It's a nice place."

"What can I do? How many permanent jobs are there in a town with just a few stores that can easily be manned by one person each?"

"There's also a woodworking shop." He turned enough to see me. "The one where you are currently employed."

"Currently being the operative word. I'm glad for the job and I do enjoy it but it was never meant to be permanent. Not really. So that leaves me back where I started. Without a job. And just as important, without a place to live because the cottage isn't habitable in the winter."

"There must be places to rent."

"Name one. Besides, there's still the problem of a permanent job. Preferably one with benefits. Which doesn't exist in Southfork."

There was silence for a long time. I could feel him thinking. I waited to hear what he'd say next but only because I was curious and not because it would make any difference. He'd be nice, I knew that. He'd be sympathetic. But once he'd thought through all possible avenues of employment and housing and realized there weren't any, then he'd agree that my prospects in Southfork were nil. And that would be the end of it.

"I've been meaning to ask you to work for me permanently."

"You don't have to do that." Because I had my pride. I'd not take charity.

"I mean it. I know it's not what you planned when you came here but I appreciate not having to do paperwork." He tipped back a bit and smiled at nothing. "And I do have more spare time now that I don't have to struggle with it myself."

"More time to fish."

"A noble pursuit and good eating."

"It's a one-person business. You said so yourself. No employees means no schedule which suits you well because you don't like schedules."

"You've adapted well to my non-schedule. I think we make a good team. And since I'm charging more for my furniture and people are happy to pay the difference I can afford you full time With benefits."

"There's still the problem of a place to live. No place to rent in town."

"We haven't looked. Maybe there is some place. An extra room. Something." He sat up and turned to see me better. "If nothing comes available I'll rent you a room in my place."

"That would be wrong." Southfork was a small town, after all, with small town mores.

"Have you seen how many bedrooms I have? Plus an extra bath? It was built for a family and I rattle around like a spare broom."

"People will talk."

He snorted. "Of course they will. People will always talk. It's what they do. A form of recreation that will mean nothing to us."

"I don't know …"

"So it's settled. Starting tomorrow you're a full time employee with benefits and when the weather gets cold you move in with me."

"Can you stand the gossip?"

There was another snort. "As to gossip, I believe it's already started due to the fact that I told the men in black that you were my wife. So there's nothing new about what people will say. Possibly by autumn they'll get tired of talking about us and find something more interesting. Like how much hay they can get put up before winter. Or if the creek will freeze completely over this year. Some years it does, other years there are open spots. In open years, swans stay all winter. If it freezes solid, they keep going south."

He paused, then added, "That's a big deal in Southfork. Whether we can watch the swans all winter or not."

I lay back in my lounge and thought about a winter with swans. They were so beautiful. Royce seemed to read my mind. "If you stay, you'll be able to watch the swans." After a pause, he added, "White swans on blue water surrounded by new snow is something you'll never forget."

That did it. Once more I spoke before knowing what I was about to say. "I'm staying. I accept your offer of a job and if I can't find a place to rent I'll be asking what you charge for one of those extra bedrooms."

"I'll make sure you can afford it on your pay."

"Which you'll know because you'll be the one writing out my paycheck."

He gave me a smug look. "Yep. It works out just fine, doesn't it?" He clasped his hands behind his head and gazed at what could be seen of the sky through the huge trees in his back yard. "You had a problem and I solved it in a matter of minutes. I'm amazing. Absolutely amazing."

We'd been sipping glasses of water. Now I leaned across the space between us and flicked some drops on him. He wiped his face clean. "What's that about? Are you picking a fight with your boss?"

"You need to be taken down a peg or two." I harrumped. "You think you're amazing? Really?!"

"I not only solved a problem, in the process I got what I wanted. In my mind that makes me amazing."

I had no answer to that and he ignored me as he

continued to stare at the sky. When he kept staring I followed his look. When he licked a finger and held it in the air, I wanted to ask what he was doing but refrained because he might decide that, too, was amazing in some way.

He dropped his hand but continued to stare at the sky. "We're due for a storm and it's going to be bad."

"No rain in the forecast. I check it every day. I don't want to leave the doors and windows open if it's going to rain. There's no air conditioning in the cottage so I like to leave them open to cool the place down. Not to mention that the fresh air smells good." I rolled over enough to see his reaction to my superior weather knowledge. "No rain. So you're not so amazing after all, Royce Adamson."

Chapter 13

"It is definitely going to rain and the more I look at that sky and feel the air around us the more certain I am that it's not just going to be a storm but that it's going to be a bad one and is going to last a long time."

I checked the sky. "No clouds. So why do you think that? What can you sense? It's just air."

"Doesn't matter. The storms will come. More than one. I can feel it."

"It's a baby blue sky."

"That will change quickly."

"You're insane."

"I'm right. I've lived in the country all my life. Rural residents know about weather. Not weather as it's doled out by forecasters who go by charts and graphs, rather we know about weather because we've learned about it the hard way. Knowing what's coming can be the difference between getting a harvest and not getting one.

"We need those harvests and we don't have pavement everywhere so we also need to prepare if we're going to be slogging through mud for weeks at a time. We know about the weather and I'm telling you that we're about to get some rain. A lot of it. And wind. Maybe you should head home and close your windows before it hits."

"If you want me to leave you can just say so You don't have to pretend a storm is coming to make me feel better about being kicked out. I'm tough. I can take it."

"I'm not trying to get rid of you. Honestly. You should know that about me by now. Knowing about the weather is a real thing. A country thing. If you stick around long enough you'll know too." He rose and pulled me up beside him. "I'd rather you stay but I know you won't want rain coming in all those open windows."

He peered down at me, those gold-brown eyes changing from dark to light and back again. "So it's best you leave now because if you stick around long enough you'll not only have rain coming in your windows you'll get wet on the way home."

I didn't know what to make of that remark. Or of anything that had happened in the last minute or so and fumed inwardly as I turned to leave because that was clearly what he expected and I wasn't about to stay where I wasn't wanted. But before I took two steps, he reached out. Grabbed me by the back of my shirt and hauled me back and turned me around until we were face to face and inches apart.

And he kissed me. Again. Of course he did. Kissing was a Royce Adamson habit that didn't mean a thing. Except this time, it did. It wasn't a quick kiss and wasn't casual at all. Not even close to what we'd shared before. It was deep and lingering and met all the criteria of the preferred kisses in the best romance books I'd ever read.

It wasn't just a meeting of the lips. It joined us in some way too deep to understand that I didn't want to dissect. There was only the lightest touch of our bodies to each other but that light touch pretty much sent electricity zinging through me and I was sure the same thing was happening with Royce.

Hands, arms, legs, thighs and every other part of us was touching just enough that something went from one of us to the other and then back again like a chain wrapping us together that got tighter and tighter the longer we stayed together even though we never moved closer to each other.

I never wanted it to end.

But Royce pulled back. When he spoke his voice was gravel and breathless and I thought he was as surprised by the kiss as I was. "You'd better get going."

My reply was the same. It wasn't my voice. It was someone else's. And I could hardly breathe. "It's not going to rain.'"

"Yes it is." He was still unable to speak normally but he gave me a light push towards the edge of his yard, touching me in spite of the electricity that charged from him to me and back. "Don't forget Cleo."

I scooped my puppy from where she was trying to dig her way to China and made my way to the road, ignoring that I'd have to chuck my clothes into the hamper because Cleo's dirty body wiggling against mine was depositing layers of dirt on everything she touched.

Halfway across the road, the rain began. It had been a cloudless sky when I looked up from that chair in Royce's yard.

How had the weather changed so abruptly?

Royce had been right. His rural weather sense had been spot-on and by the time I slammed the cottage door behind me and dropped Cleo so I could shut all the open windows, water poured from the sky in a deluge and I was soaked to the skin.

As I struggled with the last window the lightning began, followed by thunder so loud and so close that I winced and Cleo's eyes asked if she should be afraid. I made myself act normally because I didn't want a dog that was afraid of storms but if she hadn't been there I'd have cowered on the couch all wrapped up in a thick, soft blanket.

Then the wind began, howling around the cottage as if it was alive. I stayed away from the windows because I was afraid the wind would break the glass though it didn't happen. I could see out of them even from across the room and almost wished I couldn't because what I saw was every young tree in the yard bending under the force of that wind until their top branches touched the ground. It was more than a storm outside. It was elemental.

I didn't know if the TV would work and was thankful when it came on. I turned immediately to the weather channel and was greeted by a smiling, cheerful weather girl in a gold pants suit who informed me that the storm that had appeared unexpectedly was the first of a series of storms that would batter the area in the coming weeks. The ones that hadn't been expected but had appeared nevertheless.

"They are called training storms," she said brightly, smiling all the while. "Because they follow one after another like cars on a train." The smile grew wider and shone so brightly that I figured her teeth must have been recently whitened. "And they'll be bad. Just letting you know so you can prepare. Wind will also be a big thing and possible hail."

The smile drooped minutely. "And of course when there are storms like this there's always the possibility of flooding and tornadoes." She finished by admonishing her watchers to stay tuned for weather alerts. And to stay safe.

Oh joy. Would the brief walk across the road from the cottage to the woodworking shop in the morning end up with me a soggy mess because I'd not thought to bring a raincoat or umbrella when I moved to Southfork? I must get something as soon as possible. Did Lottie carry ponchos? Umbrellas? Something else?

She made sure to stock up on things tourists might need that they didn't pack because they didn't expect to need them during a vacation, like my pretty pink sweatshirt for when it had turned chilly. So there'd probably be rain coats and umbrellas for sale because no one expected rain during a vacation until the sky opened up.

I made a mental note to stop at her store the very next day during a break between downpours to buy something. I hoped the fact that Southfork didn't see many tourists meant there'd still be something available when I got there. Otherwise I'd face many soggy trips across that road in the rain.

I was thankful for Royce's non-schedule because it meant I could time going to work in the morning to coincide with a pause between storms. He'd not care if I was a bit late and if that happened then maybe – just maybe – he'd react to my belated but dry arrival with another of his trademark kisses. Out of sympathy, of course, for my journey through the rain. Or with one like the last one that hadn't been a usual Royce kiss at all.

I got to work the next morning without getting wet. In fact, the sky was blue during my dash across the road and the only evidence of the night's storm were branches littering the ground and the fact that everything outside was soaked. Cleo wanted to roll in the mud so I kept her in the office with me all day long. She didn't like it but she couldn't open the door so she stayed safe and dry.

If I'd have gone to work even ten minutes later than when I went I'd have gotten drenched. The weather girl was right. One storm after another, she'd said, and the early sun while I carried Cleo across the road was followed by a storm that darkened the world and lasted all day and, though it didn't equal the one of the previous night, it was intimidating in its own right.

"Looks like we're in for a stretch of bad weather," was Royce's off-hand remark as I deposited Cleo onto her old towels and he leaned down and kissed me. This time we were both careful. The only part of our bodies that touched were our lips and we separated immediately.

It was as chaste as any kiss could be and as soon as our lips no longer touched we got to work, Royce in the shop gluing together some rather dark looking boards that might have been black walnut into a rectangle that would become a piece of furniture while I paid the week's bills. The usual stuff.

Royce donned a poncho that hung on a hook by the back door and made a quick run to his house and brought back lunch for us and for Cleo. We finished the day's work in record time as I considered the weather beyond the single window in the office. It still rained.

"I'll work late if it's okay with you," I told Royce as he prepared to leave for the day.

"You're sure?" He followed my gaze. "You can borrow my poncho. My house is close and the trees provide some protection from the rain but you have farther to go and there are no trees."

"It looks like it's letting up so I figure if I wait a bit it'll be clear. Then I want to stop by Lottie's store and get a poncho. Or rain coat. Or umbrella. The store is next door and the overhang will keep me dry."

"If you're sure."

"I'm sure." I pointed to the papers spread across the desk. "A little more time here and I'll finish what I'm doing. So you can go home and don't worry about me." He nodded and left and I turned back to my work while Cleo slept as only a puppy can.

I was right about the rain. It did let up enough that when I closed the books, the rain was just a misty veil, both small drops coming down from the sky and haze coming up from the ground, turning the outside world into a thing of mystery. I smiled at the thought because Southfork was the epitome of rural America and as mysterious as apple pie.

Chapter 14

Lottie did have an assortment of rain gear. "Ponchos mostly because one size fits all and tourists can buy them by the dozen and distribute them to everyone no matter what size they wear." She leaned over the counter to give Cleo a pet. Or two. Or three. "But I also have raincoats and umbrellas." Cleo blinked and Lottie was smitten instantly. "I suggest not an umbrella because there's a lot of wind with these storms and umbrellas are notorious for flying away."

I took her advice and chose a bright pink poncho. "You got a thing for pink?" she asked as she handed it to me after a quick glance outside where the mist was already turning once again into a real rain. I'd clearly gotten the poncho just in time. She lolled against the counter. "And what's with you and Royce?"

"I like pink," I said as I flipped the poncho over my head with Cleo underneath against my body.

"Don't prevaricate. You like Royce. And he likes you." She sighed. "Isn't love grand?"

"It's not like that." My face grew warm. "Royce is a very friendly guy, that's all. You know the type. All touchy feely."

"Royce?" Lottie's eyebrows shot up. "Not the

Royce Adamson who lives in Southfork. He's the most conservative man I know. A bit shy. When he was in school he was considered a prude. Still is. Touch-me-not. The opposite of touchy feely."

I spoke without thinking. "He must have changed since then."

"Hmmmm." She examined me. "Tell me more."

"There's nothing more to say. Just that his kisses are the casual kind."

"Kissses? You're using the word kisses and Royce in the same sentence?" Lottie pulled back and crossed her arms in front of her. "Honey, he's not the kissing type. Never was and isn't now. When we have a barbecue, which we do now and then, everyone else is kissing and hugging, but not Royce. He's just not comfortable kissing anyone, not even his grandmother. I think he'd blush if anyone gave him a casual kiss and he'd surely not kiss anyone unless there was a very important reason. Not at all."

I nearly dropped my new pink poncho and simply had to get out of there. Then I'd need to isolate myself in my cute cottage to think over what she'd said. So I held Cleo tight and left Lottie's store as quickly as good manners allowed and dashed across the road to my cottage where I dropped my puppy to the floor, the poncho over the bathtub, and myself to a couch and just sat. And thought.

I didn't think things through, though. Not about Royce and me. I couldn't. I was too stunned. In fact I didn't think a single thought all that night and Cleo had to climb onto my lap and tell me she was hungry or she'd not have had dinner at all.

Lottie knew Royce Adamson so she'd know

whether he gave out casual kisses or not. So what was behind the ones he'd given me? I didn't sleep all night.

The next morning when I went to work it wasn't raining and Lottie was lounging in front of her store. She waved me over so instead of going straight to the woodworking shop I went to see what she wanted.

"I've been thinking." She invited me inside which meant she'd been intentionally waiting for me. I followed her in. "About the cottage you're renting."

Not about Royce. I was relieved because I didn't know what I'd say if he was to be the topic of conversation. "What about the cottage? I love it."

"It's a nice summer cottage on the banks of the south fork of a river and that's what I wanted to talk to you about. The fact that the cottage is close to the river."

"That's one of its charms."

"It's also what makes it dangerous."

"How so?"

"All this rain. It's been years since it's rained this much but the last time it did the cottage flooded and it will again if the creek rises enough to spill over its banks."

"Do you think that's likely?"

"Hard to tell. It's not just the rain we are getting here, it's also the rain upstream that will raise the level of the river somewhere else and then come downstream. It's not high enough yet, I don't think, but it can happen. What I'm saying is you should watch the creek."

"What do I look for?"

"Just check the river daily. Several times a day so you'll know before it floods and your pretty little cottage is in a pool of water with you in it. If the creek starts to overflow the banks you get out of there fast. Don't stop to pack. Nothing. Just leave."

"I have nowhere to go."

"You can stay with me. Or Royce. Or anyone in town."

"Surely there will be time to pack."

"Maybe, maybe not. You could have hours or just minutes. So if it starts to rise fast enough that you can see it creeping over the bank get out of there immediately."

I was thoughtful when I went to work. Royce noticed and I told him what Lottie had said. "She's right. I've been thinking the same thing. The cottage never became a normal house because of the possibility of floods. It's cheaper to rebuild something that's flimsy to start with and it's been rebuilt once already because of a flood a long time ago."

"Should I be scared?"

"Not if you're careful." He frowned. "Though nights are a problem. You can't check the creek in the dark." He raked a hand through his hair. "So maybe you shouldn't sleep there."

I laughed though there was no humor in the sound. "So where should I sleep? In the middle of the road?"

"At my place. Or Lottie's. Or I can drag a cot to the office and you can sleep here. You can do everything else in the cottage. Shower, eat, watch TV. But spend your nights somewhere safe."

"That's being too cautious."

He sighed. "Suit yourself." His lips pressed together. "But I'll bring that cot over today so it'll be available for you to use."

"I don't think that'll be necessary."

"It will be when you check the creek and are scared out of your mind by what you see."

"It's a creek, not some roaring river. We wade in it when we fish. It's not deep enough for swimming."

"When it overflows the banks it'll be not just deeper but different. It won't be a sleepy little creek anymore. It'll flow faster. The current will push harder. The danger will be more than you can imagine until you actually see it. You'll know what I'm talking about if it happens. If it does, get out of there as fast as possible."

I might not have believed him if Lottie hadn't already said the same thing and when I returned home that evening, wearing the poncho with Cleo safe and dry under it and against my body because the rain hadn't let up all day, I checked the creek before I went inside but it was the same, sleepy, tinkling creek of my first day in town. A few inches higher, maybe, but nothing like what Royce had described.

The next day, after checking the creek and crossing the road without a poncho because we were between rainstorms, Royce informed me we wouldn't be working in the shop. "The garden is a disaster after all the rain. We should save what we can."

The storms had turned the fenced area into a muddy morass. Clad in knee high boots and wearing rubber gloves we harvested what was viable and left the rest to die a soggy death. "We'll deal with the remains when it's dried out enough to be dirt instead of mud."

"Can we plant again when it's dry?"

"It's too late in the season but we got a lot of veggies today. Your radishes turned out to be the best crop because they came in early."

"We put in a lot of work for nothing."

"You sound like a true farmer."

"I'm learning fast."

Then it happened again. One of Royce's casual kisses. Right there in the mud without touching because if we'd touched we'd be spreading mud all over us. Royce kissed me and even as I closed my eyes and leaned into it I wondered if Lottie was right and this wasn't what Royce did with everyone he met. If it was just me. I found myself hoping Lottie was telling the truth.

"Time for lunch," Royce said as he pulled back and turned away. For the first time I wondered if he did that because he didn't know what to do next instead of because it was no big deal. I followed him into his house where we washed the fairly decent amount of produce we'd salvaged and put most of it in the refrigerator. "How about sandwiches for lunch and we spend the rest of the afternoon making vegetable soup as a last hurrah for the garden veggies?"

"We can have the soup for supper." We ate most dinners together. It was practical after working together all day.

So we chopped and stirred and tasted and added chicken and seasonings and ended up with a huge pot of soup. Royce considered it. "There's enough to feed the entire town." He looked a question at me. "Should we call everyone and have a harvest celebration of soup from our very own garden even though it's the middle of summer?"

The town of Southfork didn't have enough residents to fill a smallish church but they filled Royce's family sized house. When the kitchen grew crowded some of the excess people meandered into the dining room while others congregated on the back porch where they watched it rain.

Everyone found a place to plunk themselves down and enjoy a soup dinner complete with biscuits I'd made to go with the soup and chocolate cake afterwards that they commented on because Royce couldn't bake a decent anything if his life depended on it.

"Good thing you're here," an elderly man with whiskers said. "Royce needs you in his life if he's ever to have a decent dessert. I was afraid I'd have to go home to enjoy a piece of cake." He helped himself to a second slice as I breathed a sigh of relief that at least I'd made enough for the entire town. Village. Crossroads. Whatever it was.

We spent the next several days working steadily in the shop with me making good use of the pink poncho whenever it rained which was most of the time because that weather girl had been right. A storm would be followed by a day of beautiful sunny weather and then another storm would come that would be as bad or worse than the one before and each storm seemed to last longer than the previous one.

The creek was no longer a thing of blue water rippling over rocks that belonged in a book of poetry. Instead it was slowly gathering strength and size and morphing into something I didn't recognize. Something scary but not yet to the point of me deciding to move out. I kept Cleo on a leash out of fear that she might fall in and be swept away. And I took to checking the creek every hour or so and watching the sky as Royce was wont to do.

I didn't have his weather sense and had no idea

what to look for in the sleepy summer sky with puffy white clouds drifting along. Nor did I know what to make of the dark and scary days and nights when the rain came and the wind blew and it seemed like it would never end.

The day came that Royce got caught up on his furniture orders and I did the same with the paperwork because the weather hadn't allowed for anything to be done outside so we'd worked steadily. If it didn't rain, the mud that was everywhere prevented anyone from straying from the single gravel road that was Southfork's main street. And there was only so much window shopping a person can do in a town that consisted of a handful of stores and a woodworking shop.

So the day came that Royce said, "We're going shopping."

"For what?" I thought he'd say he needed more wood and the closest lumber yard was two towns away. But that wasn't what he suggested.

"Vegetables. I didn't stock up because we had a garden. 'Had' being the operative word."

"So we're making a trip to another town for vegetables?" So why'd we host a vegetable soup dinner for the entire town? I decided it must be a small-town thing I'd never understand if I lived there forever.

"We can do something while we're there to make the trip worthwhile. See a movie. Eat in a restaurant. Visit a bar and listen to canned music. Maybe even dance. You know, do something we can't do in Southfork because tiny villages, for all their pluses, don't have big city entertainment. And there will be actual wide concrete sidewalks so we can take a walk in the rain if we choose. No mud."

"Sounds good to me." I looked at Cleo. "Can she come?"

"We'll make a nest for her in the truck. Lots of towels and we'll leave the window part way open."

Chapter 15

The next day we took the pickup to the nearest town large enough to have more than one grocery store. It felt odd being surrounded by so many people. I'd got used to a tiny hamlet. With cement sidewalks, there were shoppers walking about even in the rain wearing ponchos or beneath umbrellas. But everyone needs food and it had been raining for so long that walking in the rain was acceptable and no one waited until it ended.

I was glad for the rain because, strolling along the sidewalk in my bright pink poncho beside Royce in his dull green camouflage one, I felt elegant. Rural elegant, perhaps, but special nevertheless. He noticed. "Maybe you should go back to the city and be a model."

"For a sporting goods store?" I whirled and the bright pink flared around me. "I could model ponchos."

"And waders and fly-fishing gear and I'd see you often because you'd be modeling in sporting goods stores and I'd be there too. Buying fly fishing rods and admiring you."

"I'll stick to Southfork and bookkeeping." But his words zinged through my body for entire minutes as we checked out the store windows and bought enough canned, frozen and fresh vegetables to last until

Christmas and beyond. After which we took Cleo for a walk to do her business, made sure she was settled in the back seat of the pickup once more, and went looking for something to do that we couldn't do in Southfork.

The movie theatre didn't open until we'd be gone so we settled for a long, slow lunch in an actual restaurant with tablecloths and more silverware than Royce liked, judging from his expression as he stared at it with distaste. Afterwards, we ended up in a combination bar and soda fountain. "Soda fountain side for the kids and the side with the bar for their parents."

We chose a table in the middle because we didn't know which we wanted and towards the back because we weren't local and didn't want to be conspicuous.

We ordered banana splits because they were more appetizing than beer. When we were about to leave, someone went to an old piano with chipped paint in a few places and began to play. No one else paid any attention but we didn't leave because the music curled through the air and turned the place into something intimate and fun. Just what we'd been looking for.

"I remember suggesting a dance while we are here." Royce cocked his head in an invitation. "This is our only chance this year unless someone in Southfork tunes up and there's no celebration I know of in the near future."

He rose and I followed. On the tiny dance floor we paused long enough to ascertain what kind of music it was. Royce kind of smiled when he recognized the rhythm. "Thank goodness. I know how to waltz." And soon we were dancing.

Not whirling around the dance floor like a couple

of professionals, rather we just kind of moved in place to the music. But it was nice. More than nice. In fact it was pretty much like his kisses. Casual or not casual and I didn't know which.

Nor did I know what Royce felt as his arms held me close and then closer still any more than I'd known how he felt during those casual kisses that could have been thrown my way without thought or could have been totally intentional and as romantic as anyone could want.

I hoped I wasn't burning him with the flames I was sure were leaping from me to him and then in every direction possible until I feared the place would catch on fire. The man holding me was that potent and I'd have groaned except he'd ask what was wrong and I'd not be able to explain.

When the waltz ended we left and returned to the light misty rain that was what often happened between the downpours and the occasional bright, sunshiny days that were the summer. Royce's arm was still wrapped around my waist. I wondered if he'd forgotten to remove it after waltz or if he actually knew how close he was holding me.

He stopped walking. Drew in his breath. Pulled me closer. Turned me towards the nearby building while moving a half step ahead and blocking me from view. "Don't move. Don't look towards the street. Pretend you are checking out the store window and keep facing the building and away from the street."

Dread spiraled through me as I did what he said. I didn't dare look to see what had caused him to react so suddenly and to change from the laid-back man I knew into something I didn't recognize. An in charge alpha male.

Royce wasn't that kind of man but he was at that moment. He leaned close as if we were a couple who couldn't get enough of each other and whispered close to my ear. "They are here. The men in the black hoodies." I felt him look up and down the street. "Their black car with the tinted windows is parked nearby. We have to get past it to reach the truck." He wrapped his arm tighter around me and made sure to be between the men and myself. "Keep looking away from them."

My world became the small space between the store we were strolling past and Royce. We pretended to be lovers and hoped to be inconspicuous. But my bright pink poncho was a beacon and I knew by Royce's quiet swearing that the men in the hoodies had noticed.

"They were outside the bar where we danced."

"That doesn't mean they saw inside."

"We can't assume anything."

We continued along the sidewalk as if we were lovers out for a stroll. I didn't look towards them but could feel their eyes on me. Or on my noticeable neon pink poncho. "Anyone would look at this poncho. It doesn't mean a thing."

"We're passing the black car now. The truck is right ahead." Hope flared because we'd soon be on our way home. Then the hope was dashed. "They are following us."

"Maybe they are going to their car. You said we just passed it."

Another few agonizing seconds later Royce relaxed. I could feel it in the release of tension in his body so close to mine. "They stopped at their car.

They're getting in. You're safe."

When we were in the truck I kept the hood of my poncho over me in case they were watching. "Do you think they recognized me?"

"I don't know. I just know we're getting out of here. We'll stop on the outskirts of town for Cleo to do her business but after that we're not stopping until we're home."

I didn't drop the hood of my pink poncho until I saw Southfork ahead of us. Then I did something unexpected. I started shivering. Royce glanced towards me. "It's a reaction. That was a pretty tense situation."

"Then is when I should have been shaking. Not now, when I'm safe." I leaned towards the dash. "Do you want me to help unload?" He shook his head and said he could do it. "Then you can let me off at my cottage."

"Good idea. It's almost dark and you should check the creek while you can still see it. There's been a fair amount of rain where the creek comes from so it might be higher than expected." He slowed as he approached the stone bridge because my cottage was just beyond it. "Oh oh!" He stepped on the gas and continued on past the cottage.

Southfork was so small that the small extra distance meant he was out of town. He drove until he reached a crossroads and turned. At the next crossroads he turned again, heading back towards Southfork on a narrow gravel road instead of the larger, wider one that went through town. The one we'd arrived on.

"I saw it. They were parked near the cottage."

"The black car." Royce nodded. "They were the same guys, I'm sure of it, in spite of the tinted windows. Which means they are waiting for you."

"They saw me. They know who I am."

"You're staying with me tonight." His mouth turned grim. "No questions, no argument, no other option."

"I'm not arguing." I shrank in my seat and pulled the hood over my head again in case the men in black happened to have walked up the bank from the cottage. From there they'd be able to see the entire town of Southfork including Royce's house where we were pulling up and I'd have to walk from the truck to his house.

"Take off that poncho. If they knew it was you wearing it this afternoon then they'll recognize it now."

"It's still raining."

"My poncho is big enough for both of us. And Cleo." He glanced into the back seat where Cleo was enjoying life and the scenery out the window. She was turning into a dog that loved to travel.

Royce came around to my side of the truck. I got down as low as possible to pull the poncho over my head without being seen by anyone watching. Then I slid to the ground and into his arms as he moved his dull green poncho over me. Together we turned towards the back door as I retrieved Cleo who was happy to snuggle in my arms with both of us beneath Royce's poncho. It was crowded but, like he'd said, we all fit.

Once we were in his house I dropped Cleo to the floor. She proceeded to explore her second favorite place in the world, tail wagging, and to nibble some of the dog food Royce kept in a bowl in his kitchen beside the water dish that she knew was hers.

I stood by the door as Royce went back on the front

porch and spread his wet poncho over one of the lawn chairs he kept there to watch life passing by and weighted it down with a couple small potted plants he kept on a shelf jutting out from the railing where they could be watered by drips from the roof.

The recent rains had got them so soaked that he'd taken them into the porch itself to save them from drowning and now they were just what he needed to keep the drying poncho from blowing away in the next gust of wind that would surely come because every storm so far had included at least a little wind. Usually a lot. The weather lady was discussing the possibility of tornados. Every evening she reminded her watchers to keep posted for further updates. And to stay safe. He brought my poncho inside where it wouldn't attract attention.

"I have nothing to wear," I said as I considered the poncho dripping all over the floor. "Everything I own except what I'm wearing is in the cottage."

"You can borrow some of my stuff. It'll be big but I have some rope somewhere that you can make into a belt and if my shirts hang on you we'll pretend they are tunics."

I laughed. It felt good to laugh as strange men who wanted me for some unknown reason waited for my return for some reason I couldn't begin to guess. Royce, seeing me laugh, came to me and took my hands in his and gave me what I'd once thought of as one of his signature casual kisses.

After talking with Lottie, though, I didn't know what to think. But as the kiss lasted longer and then still longer still, I didn't care. I simply leaned into it and enjoyed the feel of our lips meeting and our bodies coming together in a light and gentle way that somehow wasn't gentle at all.

When we separated, Royce looked into my eyes and simply said, "Wow." Then he turned away and started dinner while I made chocolate chip cookies for dessert to eat on the back porch as we watched the rain come down because the sunset couldn't be seen behind the black clouds that gathered every evening that were filled with the rain that would fall during the night.

Chapter 16

The next morning Royce emptied the truck of the vegetables we'd purchased the day before. "Don't you help." He waved me back into the house. "If those guys are still around I don't want them to see you. While I'm unloading the vegetables, however, I can meander a bit and see if they are still there."

"If they are gone, then I'll help unload."

"No you won't because they might have just moved to a different location. You can come out only when I'm sure they aren't anywhere in town."

"At least the town is small. It'll only take a few minutes to find out." He agreed and donned his poncho that had dried overnight and proceeded to bring in boxes and bags of vegetables that I stored in the freezer, refrigerator or on pantry shelves. I was impressed. This small town guy had brought a cooler. I'd not have thought to do so because I was used to shopping close to home. A city thing versus his small town knowledge.

His home was definitely designed for a family judging by the amount of storage space available. Our entire trip's worth of bags and boxes didn't fill a single one of those storage places. Royce needed a family of at least a half dozen kids to justify the size of his house. More like a dozen kids with space left over for company.

"I don't see those thugs anywhere," Royce informed me when everything was unloaded and stored in its proper place. "So you can come out from hiding and get to work."

"I want to change first. Clean clothes." He shooed me away after another quick kiss that I would have thought was casual before talking with Lottie. After that talk I didn't know what to make of it but I spent the entire walk across the road with my eyes half closed so as to hold whatever emotion was roiling around inside of me as long as possible.

But even as I concentrated on that kiss I looked forward to a quick shower and a change of clothes before returning to the shop and work. Cleo came with me on her leash that she wore proudly as a sign of her importance in the world.

Before going inside I checked the water level in the creek. It was another several inches higher than before but still within its banks though, as I watched the water moving, curling and roiling until it resembled a monster from a horror movie, I began to realize what Royce and Lottie had been trying to tell me. That the creek fundamentally changed after a lot of rain.

I'd not consider wading now in the fast moving, dark water that greeted me and, as I looked up and down the creek, I saw things floating that could have done serious damage if I'd been in their way. Branches, pieces of wood that could have come from anywhere. A discarded board, perhaps, and a length of an ornamental fence torn free by rising water that had flooded the area it enclosed.

I shivered and tugged Cleo away from what I now considered a dangerous river and went inside my cute cottage. And stopped in total shock. Because someone had been there while I was gone and whomever it was had trashed everything.

Drawers were on the floor, their contents scattered. Chairs had been tipped over and the couch had been torn apart as if it might have something inside someone wanted to find. The curtains had been ripped from their hangers and the mattress was off the bed and shredded worse than the couch. The box springs were also totaled.

Cleo wanted to go to her food and water, practically the only things untouched, but I didn't let her. I was too afraid. It was no longer recognizable as my home. It was a nightmare. And after minutes of standing in the doorway and staring soundlessly at the destruction I did the first thing that came to mind. The only thing.

I slammed the door shut and ran across the road and into the woodworking shop where I flew across the room until I plowed into Royce. Then I wrapped my arms around him as tightly as possible and held on for dear life.

"Are they back? Did they see you?" I felt him looking through the door I'd left open, expecting men in black hoodies to be following and I felt his body relax when he realized that wasn't what had brought me to him in a panic. But something had.

He held me away from him and met my terror with the calm that was a part of him. "Is the creek flooding?" I shook my head. "Then what's wrong?"

I finally managed to croak, "They broke into the cottage. Everything has been destroyed."

"Was anything taken?"

"I don't know. I didn't look. I came right here."

His arms tightened around me. "We need to check but I'm going with you. I don't think they are still in town but I'm not taking any chances." He made sure Cleo had food and water and then said, "Wait here. I want to get something." He disappeared in the direction of his house.

Five minutes later he returned with a pistol tucked in his waistband. I'd never seen a more lethal looking pistol. "No sense taking chances. Do you have your cell phone? We should take pictures."

He was taking charge. Given time to come to terms with what had happened, I'd do it myself. Take charge of my life. I'd make decisions and do things though without the gun because I didn't have one. I made a mental note to get one as soon as possible.

As I melted into his sturdy body, though, I was glad not to have to do those things. Not to need to think. To plan. All I wanted to do was exactly what I'd just done. Walk straight into the safety of his arms and stay there until he took care of everything. Everything. Until the men in black hoodies were gone. Until the black car with tinted windows disappeared for good. Until there were no more questions about me.

The rain and the rising creek were also problems to be dealt with and presented their own kind of threat and I wanted those gone too. I was sick and tired of threats. There were too many.

Even though I wanted to I didn't stay in the safety of his embrace because that would be the cowardly thing to do. Instead I pretended to be normal and followed him back across the road to the cottage wearing my shocking pink poncho that called attention to itself and that anyone within eyesight couldn't help but notice and I told myself that it didn't bother me. That I was brave and not afraid. In reality I was terrified.

"There's nothing missing." Two hours later, after a thorough search of the cottage, I was able to state with authority that everything was still there.

"So what did they want?" Royce looked around once more as if an additional glance would reveal something we'd overlooked. "Not money because the money in your drawer is all over the floor."

"And I have nothing of value."

He thought a moment, taking another look at the destruction around us. "They were looking for information." He pointed to the desk drawers that had been emptied. "Your papers are scattered more than your clothes or anything else so that's what they were most interested in." He stared at me gravely. "Do you have any idea what information they might be looking for?"

I shrugged. "None."

His eyes were dark and slitted. "Maybe you should call your father."

"What's he got to do with this?"

"Maybe it's about him. He's some kind of big shot executive, isn't he?" He let that sink in. "Maybe he did something. Or knows something. And whomever did this thinks they can get to him through you."

I had my father on speed dial so in moments we were talking. A few moments more were enough to know he had nothing to hide. "No secrets. Nothing illegal or even irregular." I'd expected that answer because he'd always been scrupulously careful about where he worked and what he did.

"Nothing wrecks a career faster than walking on the wrong side of the law or even straddling the fence. Not worth it." I'd heard that many times growing up. It had been a statement of his career path and a piece of advice for me and had led to his leaving more than one job in order to stay completely clean.

"It's not about my father."

But my father wasn't about to let me face what was happening alone. His voice over the phone rang with anger. "I'm hiring a private detective." I heard the tapping of a pencil on his desk, a clear sign of intent. "Expect him any day. He'll probably have questions." Then, after a pause, "May I speak to your employer? I believe his name is Royce something-or-other."

Soon my father and Royce were deep in a conversation about how to find out what was happening and how to keep me safe. My father tried his best to handle things from his end because that's what he did while Royce politely but firmly insisted he could do more because he was on the scene.

Neither of them asked for my input. I didn't know whether that should make me laugh or cry but I considered the one half of the men that I could see, Royce, as they divided my safety between them and decided how to find out what was going on. When the call ended I had the feeling they were both satisfied that they'd handled both the men in black hoodies and me very well. And I was angry and laughing at the same time.

"Did it occur to either of you to consider me while deciding how to organize my life?"

"We weren't organizing your life." Royce scowled as his face said he'd just realized what he and my father had done. Treated me as a child. "We were planning for your safety."

He flushed a bit and tried to hide it but he couldn't. "And figuring out how to get to the bottom of whatever is happening." He raked a hand through his hair. "Because you don't have any idea what's going on and neither do I and neither does your father." He wished they'd not forgotten me in their eagerness to deal with what was happening. "We had to work out the details. Lots of details. It's a complex situation."

"And in the process you forgot me completely."

The flush turned into a full-on blush as his shoulders slumped. "Yes, we did forget you." He came close and touched my shoulder. Just touched it in a conciliatory manner. "Sorry about that."

I folded my arms across my chest. "Promise you won't forget me again?"

A hand raked his hair a second time. "No. I can't make that promise. I might get caught up in the moment again. Like I did this time." He lifted his eyebrows and stared at the ceiling instead of at me. "I hope that's okay because it wasn't meant as a macho alpha male kind of thing."

Yes it was. It was totally alpha male and as his apology found its way to me I knew that I was fine with it in spite of what I'd said because it meant I didn't have to do all those things myself. There was someone else who'd help. Two someones, my father and Royce. But I wasn't about to admit that to the tall, good looking guy standing inches from me and feeling foolish. No way. Let him sweat. It would do him good.

Chapter 17

I slept at Royce's house that night because I no longer had a usable bed in the cottage, not to mention that I'd not be able to sleep in a place that was a disaster instead of a home. And I was afraid to sleep alone on the cot in the office. Too dangerous.

Not much got done in the office the next couple of days, either, because I was too stressed out to process numbers and spreadsheets. Royce asked for my help in the shop. He could do everything himself since he'd been working alone forever but I appreciated his effort to create a normal day for me. A day spent doing physical things that didn't require thought. The smell of wood and watching rough boards turn into finished furniture was soothing and exactly what I needed though I didn't say so because I didn't want to admit out loud how frightened I was. The break-in had been scary.

The detective showed up two days later, a nice middle-aged man named Maurice in a pale blue shirt and no tie with a pistol neatly snugged beneath his casual suit jacket. He got right down to business. "Who knew you were coming to Southfork?"

"My parents. No one else."

"Are you sure? Whoever sent these thugs had to know where you are living." After I said I was sure he asked another question. "There are ways people might learn your location. Phones and computers leave a trail. Your father mentioned some online classes."

"That's true but I don't do them in my cottage because the only internet service that's dependable is here in Royce's office. So this is where I study."

"Did the guys after you come to the office at all?"

Royce and my eyes met in a sudden recognition of where this line of questioning was headed. "Yes. They came here first but Royce was suspicious of them so he said I was his wife and they left."

"This is a tiny town. I didn't see a motel or B&B. Is the cottage the only place for rent?"

Royce said it was and Maurice looked pleased. "I think that gives us a starting point. They hacked your online account and came to the building it led to, the workshop where you download your classes. When that lead didn't pan out they left and did some research. Then they returned and went to the only place in town that's for rent and they trashed it looking for whatever they are after."

He looked around the shop. "Would you show me your computer?"

Five minutes later he smashed a bug beneath his heel that had been attached to my computer and another one from Royce's. "No one locks their doors in Southfork." He spoke as if he knew about small towns. "These guys in black hoodies didn't buy your story about Susanna being your wife and they knew the person they were looking for was taking classes on a computer in this shop. So they bugged both of them.

"They probably placed the bug on your computers in the middle of the night. It only takes minutes. So they now know everything that's been said in this office. Your favorite colors if you discussed them. What you had for lunch yesterday. Most of all they know where you live."

"In the cottage that was trashed."

Thank goodness most of our conversations had been in the shop and the door to the office had been closed. But not always. "So they know I'm the Susanna they are looking for."

"I'm sure of it. Now we just have to figure out why they are so eager to get to you." I said I had no idea. "I believe you. I've done some background work and there's nothing I can find about you or your father that's suspicious." He was silent for a few moments. "Which means it's something else. Something connected to you in some way but you personally aren't what's important."

"I have no idea what that could be."

He nodded shortly. "Spend some time thinking about whatever you've been connected to lately. Jobs. Hobbies. Groups you were active in. Especially think about recent things because since their interest is recent it's most likely that whatever triggered their attention happened recently."

"I quit my job and moved to Southfork, got a job here and am taking some online classes." I wracked my brain but could think of nothing else. "My life is pretty boring." To other people, anyway.

"List the specifics of each of those things and give me a printout. What company you worked for and when you quit. List your online classes. I know about your work here so you can skip that. I'll check the others out. Maybe something will jump out at me."

Before he left, he said one more thing. "Do what you can to make sure they don't come after you again. A security system on the cottage is a good idea. I know it's a rental but you must do what you can to be safe."

Royce's eyes slitted. "She's going to stay with me." He dared me to object as he tipped his head towards the house behind the workshop. "That's my place. Lots of room. I've already offered her a place to stay but she likes her cottage. So far."

"Small town morals." Yes, he knew about small towns. Maurice studied the white, two-story farmhouse. "It looks sturdy." Sturdy being shorthand for safe.

"It was built well. Solid foundation. Thicker than normal walls. Well maintained. Could go through a medium sized tornado with no structural damage."

Maurice turned to me. "What you do is up to you but Royce's house is definitely safer than a summer cottage and you won't be alone." He looked Royce up and down, his gaze lingering on the pistol Royce now carried all the time in the holster at his waist. "And he's armed." A half smile said what Maurice thought of that particular precaution.

Then he left the workshop but he didn't leave Southfork immediately. He went through the cottage thoroughly but found nothing Royce and I hadn't already found. He visited Lottie, George and Lyle in their stores and chatted about everything and nothing, introducing himself as a friend of the family who happened to be in the area and stopped by for a visit.

They bought his story and the four of them spent a couple hours drinking coffee and talking. I was sure when he left town he knew as much about the town and its inhabitants as I did after living there for a good part of the summer.

After watching him check out Southfork and its residents, Royce and I turned back to work and got a lot accomplished in the hours remaining. I was almost emotionally ready to return to my usual job involving numbers and spreadsheets but I enjoyed working with Royce.

I liked the smell and feel of wood as we created the furniture he shipped everywhere. I liked the precision measuring that was similar to the numbers I worked with. I marveled that it was something real that I could actually feel instead of the mental constructs I was used to dealing with.

At the end of the day we swept up the wood shavings and turned out the lights and I gathered Cleo, uncertain where I should go. Royce's house or the cottage. I'd sleep at Royce's, of course, because I had no usable bed in the cottage. But other than those hours I wasn't sure where to go.

Royce put the brooms away. "Let's check the river. It seems to be getting deeper at a faster rate than ever." Which meant the cottage could be unsafe and I'd not dare spend time there.

So we snapped Cleo to her leash and went across the road, down the embankment and past the cottage to the south branch of the river that gave the town its name. I hardly recognized it. "It's much deeper."

"And the current is ugly. The creek is a thousand times more dangerous than a week ago." He backed up. "Don't go close, not even to check the water level. No sense taking chances." He turned to me. "Pack your things and bring everything to my place."

"Okay." His voice more than his words decided me. The cottage was no longer safe. "Tonight I'll bring enough for one night. Tomorrow, if you can spare me at the shop, I'll move everything to your place." I thought ahead to what that would involve. "It'll take a while because I want to clean the cottage as much as possible. It's pretty messy even after we picked up the worst of what was destroyed."

He nodded. "Okay. No work for you tomorrow. Want my help?"

I told him I could manage and gathered enough clothes from the cottage for one night. We carried those things across the road and I hung them in the bedroom at the top of the stairs that was next to the upstairs bathroom that I'd chosen as mine. As I hung one day's worth of clothes in the closet I promised myself that by the end of the next day the room would be filled with everything I owned. I'd miss my pretty country cottage but it was no longer a country dream made real.

The next morning Royce went to work in the shop while I took the garden cart and a tarp to keep my belongings dry during the trips across the road. I didn't plan on taking Cleo with me but her pathetic expression when I put on my shocking pink poncho and started towards the door without her was more than I could handle so I found her leash and together we crossed the road for the first load of many.

Cleo thought she was helpful. She knew something important was happening so she made sure to check each item I rescued from wherever it was located. The closet for those things we'd picked up from where it had been thrown when the cottage was trashed. The floor for those things we hadn't gotten around to yet. Her help slowed things down considerably but she was happy. Once again I was glad Royce didn't think about schedules the way most people did. I could indulge Cleo's wish to be helpful.

The puppy walked across the road with me for every single load, getting wetter and wetter with each trip. By the time everything was in Royce's house she was a mess but she insisted on going back with me while I cleaned the cottage. That took a long time so she had time to dry out.

She investigated every crevice and corner of my summer rental and was puzzled because it was no longer the way she'd known it. It was empty. She had lots of space to run and play and she took full advantage of that fact and sort of got used to it and stopped looking stressed. By the time the afternoon was half over the cottage was cleanish and she was thoroughly dry.

Instead of letting her walk back to Royce's place one last time and get wet in the process I carried her beneath my poncho and only when we were inside did I let her loose. She went to her pile of old towels in the kitchen that was her bed and curled up and promptly went to sleep. Even when Royce came in, done with work for the day, she remained asleep. "You two must have worked hard."

I grinned and nodded my head.

It was odd being in his house that day. I'd been there many times already. For meals. After work. To sleep after the bed in the cottage was destroyed. But always I'd known I wouldn't stay. That I had my own place to return to. That I was there for a visit. But this time was different and I didn't know how to feel. How to act. What to say.

"What do you want for dinner?" Royce felt it too, The awkwardness. "Something easy or should we go for lasagna? Lasagna is complicated. It'll be a two-person challenge."

"I'm up for it if you are." I was grateful to him for coming up with a way to get past the strangeness of us living together. Boss and employee. Or friends. Victim and protector. Or maybe something different entirely and that was why I couldn't meet his looks and jumped every time we accidentally touched. Though he did the same and knowing he was affected too was all that made me able to function normally.

We had an early meal mainly because we started cooking as soon as he arrived in order to ease the awkwardness and ate as soon as it was ready for the same reason. By the time we finished, Cleo was awake and saying she had to go outside. So I opened the door, expecting her to head for the backyard and what used to be a garden that was the place she'd chosen for her bathroom at Royce's place.

She did go to the garden and she did do her business. Then, instead of coming back inside. she ran full tilt around the house, ignoring the rain that she surely thought was normal because she was so young that rain was all she'd known in her young life and headed for the cottage across the road. I could read her reasoning. It was her home and the place we always went after being at Royce's for a while.

Chapter 18

"Cleo went to the cottage," I yelled at Royce as I started after my wayward puppy. "I'm going after her."

"She'll be wet. Bring her to the back porch." He leaned against the doorframe and crossed his arms and grinned widely as he watched me dash through the rain, bright pink poncho flapping everywhere. I must have resembled a very large flamingo and was glad for the rain because no one else was outside to see my mad dash across the road.

Cleo was trying to get inside the cottage. I didn't want her wandering near the creek so I went straight to the door and opened it, knowing my semi-clean cottage would now get dirty all over again. But that was preferable to her heading for the creek.

Once inside I shut the door, trapping her. She didn't mind. As far as she was concerned she was home. She checked all the corners in case something had changed since she'd been there last. A few hours ago.

I flicked a look out the window towards the creek. I'd promised to check the water level every hour or so. I'd last checked it when I started cleaning the cottage. I'd got so involved in cleaning that I'd forgotten it after that one check but it was clearly still okay because there was no creek water creeping across the yard towards the cottage.

I turned my attention to Cleo. First I wiped her clean. Her paws were so muddy I had to change the water in the bucket. Then I cleaned the rest of her, a chore that took a long time because she didn't think she needed a bath. Then I found still more rags and a pail of soapy water and began the slow task of cleaning up after her because she'd managed to leave muddy paw prints in every room and across every floor. Every. Single. One.

I forgot the time. I forgot to look out the window. The first I knew that something was wrong was when I carried a pail of dirty water from the bedroom to the kitchen to empty it and happened to glance towards the door. A smallish puddle surrounded it.

"Cleo." I dumped the water in the kitchen sink and turned to my dog. "How did you manage to get wet and dirty after I cleaned you up?" She looked at me with puppy eyes and wagged her tail so I had to give her a hug to show her that I wasn't angry.

But she should also know that she shouldn't get a house dirty so when the hugging was done I took hold of her collar and turned her towards the door with the intention of showing her the mess she'd made.

Something was wrong. During the short time I'd been lecturing Cleo the puddle had increased in size. At least it looked like it had. Perhaps it was my imagination. I dropped Cleo's collar and went to the puddle to check. Maybe I could figure out why it appeared larger when it obviously couldn't be because Cleo had been with me. No chance for her to make a bigger mess.

The puddle was definitely larger. And, as I watched, it grew still more. Not fast and not much larger but it was definitely growing. Why? I carefully stepped around it and checked the door because that seemed to be where the center of the puddle was. When I did so, I realized Cleo hadn't made the puddle. Rather water was seeping under the door.

Something inside of me squeezed so hard that I stopped breathing. Then, instead of opening the door, I went to a window and looked towards the creek. All I saw was water. No yard, no grass. Just water. The cottage was sitting in what looked like a pond. The creek had overflowed its banks and was flooding the low land where the cottage was situated.

Then I did open the door. And wished I hadn't. Water poured through the opening and soon the entire cottage was awash in inches of dirty, black, cold water. I waded through it and grabbed Cleo. We'd get wet and dirty and both of us would have to take a bath when we reached Royce's house but that was okay. We'd be safe.

I pulled my bright pink poncho over Cleo and myself and started towards the door. I didn't make it because a wave of mud came crashing through the door, trapping us in the cottage. I climbed onto a table and looked around for a way to get us both out of there.

The window on the opposite side of the house from the door was our only option and I'd have to wade through the mud to reach it. But it was large enough for me to climb through and it wasn't locked. I could do it.

I had to move the table to the window so I could climb onto it and then go through the window. It was the only way I could get through holding Cleo while wearing my poncho. But as I was about to go through, the worst possible thing happened. The cottage moved. It shifted on its foundation.

The wave of mud and water had produced enough pressure to move the entire building off of the foundation and the movement had made the table slide away from the window and the glass in the window shattered into a thousand pieces, sending them into the flooded room and turning the window into a thing of glass shards that would make it impossible for me to climb through without getting a thousand cuts and the cuts could be deadly. The shards were large and sharp.

I looked around. I was beginning to panic. I reached into my pocket for my cell phone and realized I didn't have it. I'd not thought to bring it when I went after Cleo. I was only going to retrieve my puppy. No need for a phone.

Then I did panic. But even in my panic my mind worked, looking for a way out. The only other way out was through the door that the wall of mud had destroyed. It hung on one hinge and angled across the opening. In order to get through I'd have to wrest the door free of the remaining hinge and wade through mud.

I said a short prayer and headed for the door, wishing with everything in me that I'd brought my cell phone. But I hadn't. No problem, I'd wade through the mud, pull the door free and simply walk out of the cottage and across the flooded yard to the embankment. Once I was up that embankment we'd be safe.

The mud wasn't what I'd expected. It was thick and viscous, half way between mud and mud bricks.

Each step I took ended up with me being stuck in the mud and it took forever to pull my foot free. The last steps I had to step out of my shoes in order to move forward, taking the last steps in something cold and slimy that sent a chill through me, more from fear than actual disgust.

The next task was to free the door so we could get through the opening. But before I could reach for it, the cottage shifted once more. Not much, mere inches, but enough that I was thrown into the mud. It sucked at me and I couldn't climb out.

I held Cloe close and screamed. I screamed as loudly as possible. I cried out for Royce and hoped he'd hear while knowing he wouldn't.

But he did.

As soon as the words were out of my mouth his large and comforting bulk appeared in the doorway. "You didn't come right back. I came looking." He inspected the door and reached for it. Twisted it several times. His muscles corded, his face contorted. And the door came free.

He reached for me and pulled me through, out of the mud that tried to keep me in the cottage, dragging me through it and turning the few parts of me that weren't already dirty into a foul smelling mass of hair and body because it sucked enough that he couldn't pull me out of the mud itself. Only my eyes were untouched and I hoped Cloe was okay but couldn't check.

Royce kept pulling and my shoulders came out of the mud but he didn't stop when we were through the door. He kept pulling, hauling Cleo and me through what was by then a small lake with a slippery mud bottom and all the way to the embankment. Then he gathered me under the shoulders, mud and all, and tugged me up to the road. And I finally stood up.

We stood there in the rain, letting it clean some of the mud off of us. We just stood, looking back on the cottage. It hadn't shifted much, not enough to see from the road, but the door was clearly gone and a slight current moved across the surface of the new lake. As we watched, it took the door and floated it away.

"Let's get you guys home." Royce's voice was grim. And he took my arm and walked me across the road with Cleo safely tucked beneath my poncho. I insisted we go to the back porch and not enter the house until he took a hose to me. When the poncho was fairly clean I removed it and hung it over one of the chairs we sat in to watch the evenings turn into nights. Then he hosed Cleo until she was clean and clearly angry about being subjected to such an indignity but he kept it up until she could be dried with a towel and dropped in the kitchen where she immediately went to her bed and curled up in a tight ball.

Then he tipped his head and looked at muddy me. "With clothes or without?" He held the hose and waited for my answer.

"I'll keep my underwear on." Everything else was too muddy to even think of wearing. As soon as I peeled my outerwear off I sent it straight to the garbage can at the back of the yard, not caring that the rain poured over me. It was a good start to getting clean. Then I returned and Royce hosed me off. Full power, laughing as he aimed the hose all up and down my body.

"I'll get you," I sputtered as I leaned away from the spray. Then I giggled because he'd done it on purpose to get my mind off the disaster that had once been a summer cottage.

He brought a big, fluffy, white towel. "White? Don't you have anything other than white? It'll never be white again."

"So it'll be a gray towel. Gray is a decent color."

So I wiped myself dry, surprised to find most of the mud was gone. But I still smelled and only a hot shower that lasted forever and a full bottle of liquid soap got me back to normal. By the time I was done, I'd used up all the hot water and stepped out of the shower just before the water turned cold.

I spent a long time combing my hair, toweling myself once again while knowing this towel at least would remain white, staring at myself in the mirror to see if the terror still showed or if knowing I was safe had brought me back to my usual self.

Bad men were after me. Now the weather was too. My reflection was terrified.

I finally went downstairs to where Royce waited with a pot of coffee and donuts I'd made a day earlier because he didn't bake but I did and had taken full advantage of his generous kitchen to wade through flour and sugar and cooking oil and all kinds of seasonings.

He pulled my chair out as a knight of old would do. His fingers grasped the back of the chair hard but it was only when he released it that I knew why he gripped it so tight. His hands were shaking though he tried to hide it.

I sat for a moment at the table. I took a sip of coffee and a bite of donut. Then I pushed my chair away from the table and stood up and went to where

Royce was standing, watching me. And I kissed him.

He was surprised. It had always been the other way around before. He'd always done the kissing and I'd been the recipient. But he leaned into the kiss and we stood that way for a long time until he groaned softly and pulled me to him and deepened the kiss.

Eventually he pulled away. "When I knew you were in that cottage and saw how it was detaching from its foundation and preparing to float away, you can't imagine what I thought. How scared I was."

Then he pulled me to him again and I went willingly, happily, unconcerned about what the future might bring because the present was so perfect that I couldn't think beyond it.

Chapter 19

The flood waters receded enough that there was mud instead of water where the yard used to be. The mud hid that it had shifted off its foundation. After a few days of checking the mud it was possible to slog through it to see how the cottage had fared inside. One step at a time and walking carefully so as not to let the mud suck my new boots off.

I told Royce I wanted to check things out. "It's sunny today. It's the first time in practically forever that we've had more than a few hours of sunshine at a time. If I wait for the mud to dry completely it'll turn into concrete and if there's anything in the cottage worth saving I'll have to chip it out of that concrete. So I'm going as soon as we're done in the shop." I looked at Cleo. "But I'm locking Cleo in your house so she can't follow."

I thought Royce would agree it was a good thing to check out the cottage and rescue a few things but he didn't look happy. "The cottage is an accident waiting to happen and the sunshine is temporary."

"What do you mean?"

"There are more thunderstorms coming. Nasty ones. With tornados."

"Do you think it'll flood again?"

"Not a lot of rain in the storms according to the forecast. Mostly wind. But enough to damage a flimsy cottage that's already off its foundation."

"I'll be careful. I'll keep the windows open to watch the weather. If the wind rises, I'll leave immediately."

"The door and the east window don't exist anymore." He didn't like what I planned to do. "You'll know what the weather is like if you pay attention, though, because the wind will blow right through." As I started out the door without my pink poncho because it wasn't raining his face turned dark and his lower lip stuck out. "You should be fine." But his expression said he didn't believe his own words.

He kissed me goodbye. Every time we separated lately we kissed and, as usual lately, it wasn't a chaste kiss. Or a casual one. In fact, each kiss lasted a bit longer than the previous one and though it wasn't planned by either of us, each time we kissed we came closer together and wrapped our arms harder around each other than the time before.

It was unsettling. There was nothing beyond kissing but with the deepening of those kisses there was also a deepening of emotion, though with everything going on in my life I was so emotionally unstable that I couldn't separate good emotions from bad ones, not even while kissing Royce, so I didn't know what those kisses meant, especially on Royce's end. And I wasn't brave enough to ask.

I knew what I hoped they meant but the only thing I knew for sure was that life loomed larger and larger and more and more uncertain each time we came together and if something – anything -- didn't change soon I'd go insane.

Crossing the road to the cottage I glanced towards the business part of Southfork. All one block of it. I looked for a black car with tinted windows. Or men in black hoodies. Ever since the cottage was broken into I looked for them because they'd scared me thoroughly. Every time I stepped outside. But they'd not showed up since trashing the cottage.

The sun was warm on my back as I clambered down the embankment to what used to be a yard and was now mud and debris with a cottage standing slightly ajar in the middle. I was glad for the knee high rubber boots I'd got from Lottie's store. The woman had everything anyone could possibly need, a result of many years of residents and visitors asking for stuff they didn't expect to need and discovered in an emergency that they did. Like ponchos. And rubber boots.

The inside of the cottage wasn't as bad as I expected. The floor was a disaster but the damage was limited to the bottom foot or so. I walked through the mud and opened the doors to the lower kitchen cupboards to check on their contents.

My pots and pans were intact. The ones on the bottom shelves were encased in mud so I concentrated on rescuing them first. No water to clean them with, of course, because the pipes were no longer connected to the cottage and someone had turned off the water so it wasn't flowing. I wondered if the well water was still safe. Probably not.

I found bed sheets on one of the higher shelves in the bathroom and decided to use one to carry whatever I could save but first I wiped the pots and pans as clean as I could get them with a series of washcloths from that same shelf. When I ran out of washcloths I used towels, starting with hand towels because they were small but switching to bath towels when I ran out of the hand ones.

I soon had a pile of dirty towels and washcloths to be carried in a second sheet while the actual pots and pans would be toted in the first one. When I'd done my best with pots and pans I turned to the clean dishes and silverware that had remained above the water line. They filled a third sheet.

Then I checked out the bedrooms and found the same thing. Everything below the water line required a decision as to whether it was worth saving or not. Going through each item took a long time.

With five sheets finally filled with things I'd bring to Royce's house, I decided to go back and get the garden cart I'd used to move my computer and assorted auxiliary equipment into his office when the internet connection turned out to be a disaster. Now the entire cottage qualified as a much worse disaster. I almost laughed. I was moving in with Royce one disaster at a time.

I was tired so I dropped into a chair that, thankfully, had a dry seat though the legs were lost in a mud bath. And I looked out the window with the broken glass.

And blinked.

The cottage was below the road, at the bottom of an embankment and set among large, thick trees so the wind couldn't reach it. But if it had been high enough to catch the wind then everything in the cottage would be blowing about indiscriminately. Because the storm Royce had predicted had arrived.

I went to the door to see how bad it was. The sky that had been blue and filled with sunshine when I arrived was now a sullen gray with layers of dark clouds scudding across in an angry fashion. Some went in one direction while others went elsewhere and still more were beginning to rotate.

What had Royce said? Tornados had been spotted in these storms? But what I saw were still just clouds. Not tornados. Yet.

I decided to get that garden cart and haul what I had salvaged to Royce's place and do it as quickly as possible. I'd forget about the rest until the weather calmed down. So I trudged through the muddy yard as fast as possible and up the embankment.

When I reached the road I fairly flew across it and around Royce's house to the back yard where the garden cart stood next to the garden that no longer existed. And I pulled it to the cottage and began loading it.

It wasn't easy. I had to leave the garden cart on the road because I couldn't pull it through the mud. Then I had to carry everything from the cottage, across the mud, up the embankment and to the cart. But the cart did help. It got things to Royce's faster than if I'd had to carry everything the entire distance in sheets.

I brought two loads to Royce's, leaving everything on his front porch and then returning to the cottage for the next load. I was so busy getting everything moved that I didn't bother looking up.

I should have.

When I finally checked the sky I saw a tornado

forming in the clouds directly above me. But it might not come to the ground. Most tornados didn't. I might be able to get my load safely to Royce's. I grabbed the sheet filled with my belongings tighter and started slogging across the mud.

"Drop it!" Royce's voice was close and loud and brooked no argument. I looked around and saw him coming towards me through the mud as fast as possible. No boots and why'd he come without protection from the mud? He had boots. He should have worn them.

But he wasn't done yelling. He pointed. "Look behind you!" I did as he asked and sucked in my breath. A second tornado was on the ground not far away. And coming straight towards us. "Drop it now." Royce fairly screamed. "And run!"

I dropped the sheet and watched with some other part of my mind as it sank into the mud. Then I turned, trying to decide where to go. How to run in the mud. What to do.

By then Royce had reached me. He grabbed my hand and hauled me after him. I didn't know what he was doing. Where we were going. Where we'd be safe. The tornado was coming towards us and gathering speed and strength as it came. The cottage wasn't safe. Neither was the yard. Or the embankment. The first tornado was already on the road so there was no way we could get across to Royce's house.

Then I saw where we were headed. Royce pulled me and we both struggled through the mud towards the stone bridge the creek flowed beneath. Towards a stone bench half way down the embankment for people to sit on to enjoy the view.

The tornado advanced faster than we could get

through the mud. I wanted to scream because we'd not make it but doing so would take too much effort. In moments we'd be caught up in the tornado and tossed about like confetti. At the very least, we'd be hit by the debris it had collected on its march towards the tiny hamlet of Southfork.

As I was about to give up and drop into the mud in the hope that being on the ground would save me, Royce gave one last, hard yank, sending me past him and throwing me beneath the stone bench, then slamming his body on top of mine as the tornado reached us.

His arms went around me as he grabbed the ends of the bench to hold us tight, anchoring us both to the ground and the bench as the wind arrived.

It howled, streaming hard and then harder still while clawing around and over and beside us. It was a living, breathing, screaming monster.

I pressed my face as close to the ground as possible and felt Royce press his face into my hair, both of us trying to hide from the wind. I thought we'd fail. The tornado was too strong. Too evil. I thought we'd die together and wondered hysterically if that was the logical end to all the chaste and other-than-chaste kisses we'd experienced. A shared and very chaste death by tornado.

Then the unearthly wind moved on and we were left with pink and blue and green and brown detritus that had been lifted off the ground by the tornado and was now falling slowly, gently back to the earth because the wind was gone and there was no longer anything to suspend all those multi-colored things in mid-air.

One of my pink slippers settled not far from the stone bench. A handful of shredded, green leaves fell in a scatter-shot pattern over the mud and stayed there, light as air and moving gently in the breeze that was all that remained of the wind. The sheet that had been waiting for me to haul it to the garden cart landed on the branch of a nearby tree, minus everything that had been in it, and waved gently to and fro.

And Royce slowly, painfully, as an old man, slid off of me and out from beneath the stone bench. He held out his hand. I took it and let him pull me out and up until we were both upright and looking at each other. At nothing, actually, not at each other after all, because even though we tried to focus on each other's face we couldn't.

But it was odd. We didn't have to see each other. We could simply exist. Because we each knew what the other was thinking. And feeling. And wanting because the moments beneath the stone bench when we didn't know if we'd live or die had done something to us.

Royce groaned without realizing he was making a sound and reached for me but the motion was unnecessary because I was already moving towards him. Towards his outstretched arms. Towards the sanctuary he represented because standing there beside him meant we were alive and unharmed. We could stand. We could touch one another.

Unlike all the other times, though, we didn't kiss. Instead we simply wrapped our arms around each other as the storm moved slowly away and the sun came out in time to return the day to the warmth it had begun with.

We held each other and rocked together to some

unheard music until the sun tilted towards the west and we knew the day was mostly over and we should stop dithering and move because we had things to do. A town to clean up. A puppy to care for. And lives to live.

Chapter 20

We couldn't stand forever and do nothing. We had to take stock. So we pulled apart and looked around. The cottage was gone. All that remained were boards and parts of boards everywhere. Some were in trees, others in the creek and floating away to soon become someone else's problem somewhere downstream. Still more lay in the mud where they made a boardwalk for us to follow.

"If it did this to the cottage, what's the town like?"

"Is your house still there?"

"And the workshop?"

We moved as one around the stone bench and climbed the embankment to see if Southfork had survived the tornado.

The town was still there. The buildings were all still standing. But Lottie's roof was gone. The frame was a bare bones skeleton against the sky. "There's enough left to hold tarps and protect the inside from the weather until it can be repaired," was Royce's only comment as we surveyed the damage.

The feed store was mostly intact but with much of the siding gone and scattered across the road. Except what we saw wasn't enough to account for all the missing siding so it must be distributed over several counties.

The sacks of feed that were normally stacked outside next to the front door were gone and a layer of feed covered the town. Birds that had sheltered in trees to survive the tornado were already circling above, checking it out and diving down for an easy meal.

The farm implement store was the least damaged business. The path of the tornado was easy to see from where we stood. It had almost missed the largest store in town and the rows of farm machinery in the back were untouched. The worst damage was broken glass and that could be cleared though whoever did the work would have to step carefully to avoid getting cut.

Most of the houses of the town, the most numerous buildings because it was more of a place to live than a town to shop in, were untouched, including Royce's. As was the workshop even though it was next door to the store that had sustained the most damage. Lottie's place.

Some houses were missing porches or had holes in their roofs, while the siding on others had been blown away. There were branches and leaves everywhere. The road was impassable. But the houses themselves seemed mostly undamaged, which meant the people inside of them should be unhurt.

We stared at Royce's untouched house. "Cleo will be okay." He squeezed my hand to acknowledge my concern.

As we watched, Lottie stepped out of what was left of her store. The roof had blown away with her inside and she was in shock much as Royce and I had been after sheltering beneath the stone bench. She stood in front of her store and looked around. And looked some more. But she saw nothing. Heard nothing. She just stood there.

We moved as one person to see what we could do. If we could bring her back to the real world. We reached her and the three of us surveyed the damage without being able to bring ourselves to do anything. There was too much. No place to start. We were overwhelmed and not over our shock. Soon we were joined by George and Lyle who also stared at nothing and everything as we all tried to come to grips with what had happened.

Then the residents of Southfork came from their houses, one at a time, slowly, looking this way and that as they tried to take in what had happened. They'd not had the damage the business sector had and they weren't in such severe shock.

One man rubbed his hands together and said, "Let's get started." Another said he had a Bobcat but someone else said we should take pictures first. "For insurance."

That was followed by a laugh with no humor. "And for the news media."

As his words died, a sound drifted on the wind. A roaring. It was so much like the tornado that we all tensed until a helicopter appeared, at first small and far away but soon large and looking for a place to land. When it set down on the edge of the business district we could read the logo on its side. "The media have arrived."

Another wry comment was made. "Guess this is what it takes to get a tiny place like Southfork in the news." As the words died, a second helicopter appeared and, like the first, grew larger and louder until it, too, landed beside the first and a reporter and photographer climbed out.

Soon news vans came tearing down the road and even before we could begin cleaning up, Southfork was prime time news, complete with reels and pictures of all of us against buildings that were partly or mostly gone. And all of those media people wanted heart-rending stories to accompany the pictures.

Lottie pointed to me. "Talk to her. Her cottage was blown to smithereens and she barely got out alive." She pivoted and pointed to Royce. "That's Royce. Her boyfriend. He saved her. Risked his own life to do so."

She smiled, slowly coming back from the dark place she'd been in. "He didn't have to do anything. He was safe. But he did. Ran straight at the tornado when he saw it coming 'cause she was in its path and he had to save her. He could have died. They both could have."

When Lottie finished speaking the entire contingent of media types came to where Royce and I stood, fighting to get close to us and be the first to ask questions and take pictures.

They took a lot of pictures. And asked a lot of questions. And raced each other across the road to take still more pictures of what was left of the cottage and the overflowing creek with detritus hurtling along on the crest of the current.

Then they returned and took more pictures of me. And of Royce. And of Royce holding me as he'd been doing when they first arrived, with his arms around me and pulling me against his back. Upon hearing the details of our survival they rushed back across the road still again to take pictures of the stone bench that had saved our lives. And of the stone bridge that was a hallmark of Southfork. And then of the town itself because it was a quaint and very photogenic piece of rural America that looked as if it was under attack.

Some of the media types left as soon as they had pictures and names to go with the pictures. Others remained because they wanted the story behind the headlines. The back story, they called it. And they wanted that story to feature me because I was the resident of Southfork who'd lived in the one building that had been both flooded and then obliterated by a tornado and was lucky to have survived.

Royce added spice to the story, partly because I worked for him and partly because he saved my life but mostly because they had pictures of him with his arms wrapped around me as if we were lovers. Love was great for the evening news.

Soon all of us, reporters and residents alike, trooped into the feed store. The reporters sat around that huge table with coffee and donuts littering the tabletop as I was interviewed while the Southfork residents stood behind and listened because this was the most exciting thing that had happened in the tiny hamlet as far back as anyone could remember. And the worst.

The media types checked out the feed store and took dozens of pictures filled with gobs of country charm to add to their stories as they asked a thousand questions and slowly learned everything about the town. And about me.

They soon knew I'd moved to Southfork after quitting a job in the city. That I'd ended up working for Royce. They learned how great the creek was for fishing when it wasn't in a flood stage and how Royce and I often fished together in addition to working together in addition to living in the same house when the weather was threatening. And on and on and on until I was tired of their questions and wanted to go home. To Royce's home. Not the cottage. Because his house was the only home I had now that mine was gone.

They finally left and everyone went back to their own houses because it was too late to do much cleanup that day. Tomorrow, everyone said. Tomorrow we'd get started. Tonight everyone wanted to watch their TVs and check their internet news to see if they could see themselves in the stories featuring the tornado.

After watching the news, they told each other, they'd adjourn to their porches as usual and sit in the warm, dark summer night and enjoy the night sounds against the background of the rural stillness and peace they'd known all their lives. The peace that returned after the media types left. And they'd simply give thanks that they were alive.

Royce and I did the same thing after making sure Cleo was okay and feeding her and taking her for a walk along the back of the yard and around the non-garden that hadn't been touched by the tornado.

We had toasted cheese sandwiches and canned tomato soup for dinner because that was all we had the energy to prepare. We found ice cream in Royce's freezer that we brought onto his back porch and ate while sitting on the swing that Royce pushed back and forth with one foot while we watched the night.

"You are famous," he finally said in a voice soft enough not to break the mood that had slowly wrapped around us. Frissons of feeling ran amok along and through my body but I didn't know if they were good feelings or remnants of the terror of the tornado. I was that emotionally lost that I couldn't tell the difference.

"You were on all the TV stations and all over the internet." He finished his ice cream and set his bowl on the porch railing to be brought inside later. "Everyone in America now knows your name." He tested my name, rolling it on his tongue. "Susanna." He turned to me. "That's you. Susanna Brown of Southfork, survivor of not just one but two natural disasters."

I reminded him of the thing we'd not told the reporters. "I also survived being spied on by a bunch of men in black hoodies."

The swing had stopped when he'd finished his ice cream and put the bowl on the railing. Now he took my empty bowl and placed it beside his. Then he pushed the swing into gentle motion once more. "I hope those guys in black don't watch the news but I'm sure they do. If they didn't know who you were before the tornado nearly took out Southfork, they do now."

He moved closer as if mention of the men in black had resurrected his protective instincts. "I wonder if all this publicity will chase them away for good. Or if it'll bring them running back because now they know for sure who you are. Most of all, I wonder what it is about you that they find so interesting."

He wrapped an arm around me, pulling me close. And then closer still. "Whichever of those things it is, don't worry. I'll have your back." Then he kissed me and just like that we were once more our usual selves, the selves from before the tornado. Except with the difference that the tornado had accelerated whatever was growing between us, the thing that I couldn't identify beyond that I liked it.

It was frustrating. I didn't know how to feel. It was as if my body no longer belonged to me. As if I didn't know who I was. What I felt. I only knew that when Royce was nearby I felt right. Good. But even as I felt that way I also felt like someone other than the person I'd been before I moved to Southfork. I was changed and the change was happening so very fast. I didn't know how to handle it.

So I did the only thing I could figure to do. I let Royce take charge. I followed his lead and as the swing slowed and stopped and he leaned into our kiss and I responded with everything in me I accepted without any reservations whatsoever that wherever he was headed, whatever that place was that he saw in the distance, I'd go there with him.

Chapter 21

Was I in love? I'd never been in love. Never had a real crush on anyone, never had a serious boyfriend. Never known heartbreak. Still wasn't sure if my roller coaster emotions were good or bad. But I thought good. Probably.

The thing was, I didn't know if what I was feeling was love or maybe just something close but not the real thing. It felt real, like the best of every romance I'd ever read when I should have been doing something else. But how to know for sure?

Most of all, though, I didn't know what Royce's feelings were towards me and that made things truly weird as we sat in the dark and watched the night and kissed and moved our bodies subtly against each other so as to better experience whatever was happening while Cleo slept in the kitchen and the town of Southfork faced the fact that life would never again be exactly as before the tornado struck.

Silence felt right in that warm darkness so we didn't speak. Not a word. Not about the tornado. Not about us. Not about anything. Instead we simply sat on that swing as Royce pushed it slowly back and forth while we learned about each other in a very personal way and I wondered whether what we were doing was a physical reaction to what had happened that day and all the days leading up to it. Or something different. Something deep and elemental.

When the moon had moved far enough across the sky to remind us we'd been there just about forever we went inside in that same total silence and climbed the stairs to our respective rooms silently and shut the doors without saying good-night or good-bye to each other. And so we let the day come to an end without either of us acknowledging – anything.

The sum of what had just happened – or not happened – was that I'd cry all night and not sleep a wink even though I was worn out. Exhausted. It had been an extraordinary day and the days before the tornado hadn't been exactly peaceful either and now I didn't know how Royce felt about me or much of anything at all.

All those things added up to more angst than I could handle and everyone knows it's impossible to sleep after severe trauma. So I pulled the blankets tight around my shoulders and prepared to spend the night reliving everything and thinking about Royce and crying until my pillow was wet and I had no more tears left.

Silly expectation. I was out like a light as soon as my head hit the pillow.

The next day even before breakfast we heard unidentifiable sounds in the direction of the businesses that had been hit by the tornado. Munching on donuts and drinking coffee Royce had made before I came downstairs, we went outside and checked those sounds out.

We saw Bobcats grabbing pieces of buildings that were lying everywhere on the ground and dumping them into trucks that hauled them elsewhere. We heard the thunder of equipment and the hum of machinery.

More than equipment, though, there were people. They were everywhere, hoards of them, and they were cleaning up Southfork one piece of debris at a time, picking things up from the ground and pulling them out of trees and retrieving them from under more debris. If whatever they found might be something of value they added it to one of several piles to be gone through and eventually returned to its rightful owner.

The piles were small, though, because the houses were relatively intact so they consisted mostly of things that had been in yards or on porches when the tornado struck. Lottie was going through them to find items from her store that might be salvageable. She waved to us. "I'm going to have the storm sale to end all storm sales." The shock was gone. She was semi normal and she used an arm to wipe sweat from her forehead. "Depending on how the insurance works out, of course."

She stood beside a pile of ponchos though none were shocking pink because I'd bought the only one she had. But there were green and blue and purple ponchos and a pile of rubber boots waiting to be sorted into pairs. "I can help."

She waved me away. "Wait until I hear from the insurance company. They are sending someone ASAP."

So we kept walking, looking for a way to help but those hoards of workers had arrived with the rising sun and immediately organized themselves into teams. My father would have approved. It was America on steroids.

My cell buzzed. It was my father. "Glad you're alive." Cryptic as usual when he was trying to hide his feelings. My mother's voice in the background conveyed the emotion he tried to avoid as she said we should have called them while also saying she knew I'd been beyond doing anything at the time but now that I'd had a night's rest could I please tell them all about how I almost died.

Royce led the way to the stone bridge and we sat there and watched the brown, roiling water flowing below as I described the previous day's events. There was silence on the other end as my parents absorbed what had happened while they'd had another normal day at work and at home. Then my father cleared his throat and I knew there was another reason for the call.

" Maurice got back to me." He cleared his throat. "The detective."

"Did he find out anything?"

"He did and now we know who is asking about you and why."

"Tell me, please."

I set my phone to speaker so Royce could also hear what he had to say. "It's as I thought. Organized crime. The mafia."

"That makes no sense."

"It actually does. It goes back to that exit interview from your last job."

"The company that makes toys."

"And stuffs drugs into those toys and ships them everywhere." He waited for me to internalize his words. "There must have been something about that exit interview that made your former bosses think you'd found out about their drug business. They aren't the biggest players in town but they are ambitious and willing to take out anyone they think might mess with their business. So they decided to silence you and were merely waiting to make sure they offed the right woman."

I sagged and might have fallen had Royce not grabbed me. "That exit interview." I found myself talking without thinking. "They were nasty. I got angry. They mentioned the NDA I signed and I said something about it not being important unless they did things that are illegal."

"That must have been it. They thought you were letting them know you were on to their illegal activities."

"I didn't mean it. I was just being nasty back."

After a long pause, my father said, "Don't worry, Susanna. We'll handle it."

"How?" I looked at the sky and at Royce. His face was a mask of shock.

"Maurice is contacting law enforcement as we speak. They'll take over and put those crooks out of business and then you'll be safe."

"If it was that easy why didn't they do so before now?"

"There is currently no proof and that company was just one of many they are investigating. They were pretty sure they were selling illegal drugs but they could have been legitimate."

"There's still no proof. I didn't even know about it until you told me just now."

"Because of what's happening to you they now know there truly is drug trafficking so they'll dig deeper. Deep enough to find proof and put them out of business. Then you'll be safe."

"And in the meantime?"

Another long pause was followed by, "In the meantime, you've got Royce. And all of Southfork."

Royce spoke. "Don't worry, Mr. Brown. Susanna will be safe." His voice was changed. Different. Angry. And determined. A thrill went along my spine because I believed him. I'd be safe because Royce Adamson would make sure I was.

As usual, when I clicked my phone off and slipped it in my pocket and Royce could let me go because I was once more capable of sitting and standing on my own, before he let loose of me he kissed me. Again. As he'd done a hundred times already.

But this time I didn't just respond quietly. As his lips left mine, I thought back over the things that had happened to me lately and decided I was tired of being set on the shelf and taken care of like a child.

I stared straight at him. "Royce, I've had enough. I am presently being jerked around by a bunch of criminals. I almost drowned when my cottage was flooded. I was just about blown away by a tornado. And now I'm being kissed by a guy who happens to be the best fly fisherman in the county and who could pass for a male model and he's jerking me around just like those criminals are doing and like the weather tried to do."

He blinked. His mouth stayed open as if he didn't know how to shut it. "What are you talking about?"

"You." I stuck a finger at his chest. He looked down at it as if unable to figure out why it was there. "I'm talking about you, Royce Adamson. You."

"What am I doing wrong?" He turned red. "Was it

the kiss? Don't you like being kissed?" He turned redder still. "I'm sorry if you don't like it. I thought you did. You never said anything before now."

"I do like it."

"Then what's the problem?"

"The problem is that I don't know why you are kissing me. I don't know whether it means you like me or you love me or just that you're bored and have nothing better to do with your time so a kiss or two will do until something more interesting happens." I took my finger off his chest and hugged myself. "Or if kissing is just your thing and it means nothing at all."

I could feel tears starting and I prayed for them not to fall but knew they probably would anyway. His mouth snapped shut. "Kissing is not my thing." He withdrew his arms and moved slightly away from me. "I don't kiss casually." His brows knit. "Why would you think that?"

"Why wouldn't I? You've given me no reason to think differently."

He was insulted. I could see it in those brown-gold eyes. They sparked. His cheeks puffed out. His shoulders tensed. He raked a hand through his hair as he always did when he was under stress. Then his eyes narrowed and he leaned close to me and I knew he'd come to some kind of decision.

And he kissed me. Again. He pulled me so close I thought I'd not be able to breathe, wrapping his arms around me and hauling me onto his lap and pretty much surrounding me with himself. I quickly learned what a real Royce kiss was like and it was nothing like all the ones that had gone before. It was a thousand times better, deeper, sweeter and lasted way longer and turned me to jelly. It also told me a whole lot about Royce Adamson.

When he put me away from him and we came back to the world his voice was husky. "Was that better?"

I answered when I, too, could manage to speak. "Much better."

"Was it satisfying?"

"Very satisfying."

"Did it answer any questions you may have about my intentions?"

I tipped my head in thought. "Yes, but I still want to hear the words."

He touched my forehead with his own and groaned. "You're going to make me say it, aren't you?"

"Yes."

"Okay." Those ever-changing eyes turned dark as he gathered his thoughts. "Okay. Here goes. I love you and I want to marry you. So will you marry me?" His lower lip stuck out. "Is that good enough? Plain enough? Did you get the message?"

"Yes it's plain enough and yes I'll marry you."

"You will?" Surprise swept across his face. "Really?"

"Yes. Really. If you want me to." I inspected that surprised face. "Now that I'm looking at you, though, I'm not sure you mean it. You look – uncertain."

"Of course I mean it." His eyes grew even darker until they were night and golden stars. "I'm just surprised, that's all. You're a city girl and I'm a country guy. Why would you trade what you had before for Southfork and me?"

I giggled. "I like small towns. But most important is that Southfork is where you are. So I'm a fan of

Southfork and you. It's a package deal."

He thought that through. Then he smiled. Then he laughed quietly. "Okay. Now there's just one more thing to be done before we get our happily ever after."

"What's that?"

"See if Lottie carries Susanna sized bubble wrap to keep you safe until those drug dealers are caught and we can stop worrying about thugs in black hoodies."

"I don't need bubble wrap."

"I think you do."

We left it at that because Lottie didn't carry bubble wrap and we had things to do. A business to run when the fish weren't biting, a puppy to walk and plans to make.

Chapter 22

No one was surprised when we announced our engagement. Absolutely no one, not even my parents. My father, the city person, just said in his best I-can-survive-anything voice, "I suppose the wedding will be in Southfork." Adding, in a voice that struggled to sound happy, "It's a lovely small town."

He finished with, "Your grandparents will love it. Probably stick around until the snow flies." Because, unlike my city-loving parents, they were small town people. "I suspect once you are wed they'll visit often." As would my parents but they might not stay as long.

We didn't get married immediately even though we wanted to, mostly because Lottie didn't carry the bubble wrap Royce insisted was essential to my safety and the authorities hadn't yet arrested my former employers and we didn't want to call attention to my existence any more than the media already had. As Royce said, "Even if it's not a big wedding that would normally be in the city papers, it might be featured there anyway because your father is a big shot executive."

He continued with, "But if we wait long enough and there's no publicity of any kind then maybe those thugs will have forgotten about you." He didn't sound hopeful. "Then I can stop wearing a pistol everywhere I go. I clean it every day to make sure it's not clogged with sawdust."

"I'm sure you don't need to wear it in the shop."

He looked at me warily. "Those guys were at the shop once already. I'm not taking any chances."

He wore that pistol because of me. He said he'd wear it forever if need be but I felt guilty every time he strapped it on before we left the house, even if we were merely going to the shop that was just across the alley.

For that same reason I didn't go to town even though town was next door to the shop where I worked. A dozen or so steps. But I didn't take those steps because now that we knew who'd been asking about me and why they targeted me the knowledge was enough to kill any desire I might have to leave the safety of Royce's house.

The only places I felt safe were in the shop and his house and yard. Cleo needed her exercise and to be walked to do her business and I was comfortable playing with her and following her around the yard. My goal was to help her learn the boundaries of her world. The fenced in garden at one end and Royce's house at the other and the edges of the lawn on the sides. She wanted to explore the longer weed-filled spaces on either side but I made sure she understood those weeds were stretching the limits of her allowed space.

Mornings began with me nibbling on a donut as I drank the coffee Royce always had made by the time I came downstairs. "If the authorities don't catch those thieves soon I'm going to be an old maid." I looked out the window at the green leaves that held the slightest hint of the deeper, less shiny green that preceded autumn.

"They're working on it."

"If it doesn't happen soon we're having a wedding anyway no matter the danger." I looked into Royce's face and loved the grin that started in his eyes and soon took over every part of him. He loved knowing I wanted him and that we both were tired of waiting. "A small one, maybe, but a wedding."

"With a white dress and flowers and all that wedding type stuff?"

"I have the dress ordered and everything figured out so the instant we get the word they are in jail we're heading for the church just outside of town." An old-fashioned white church with a soaring steeple that wasn't in town because, as Royce explained, a hundred or so years ago a farmer had built it himself on his property so he could walk across his yard to attend church instead of hitching up his team and driving into town.

And it was still there. "The thugs don't know it exists and might not find it if they came looking. It's in a thick grove of trees."

"We're not taking chances. Not yet." My reward for my suggestion was another of Royce's kisses and since I finally knew the full extent of the feelings behind those kisses, I lapsed into silence and tried to be content.

At that moment, Cleo said she needed to go outside and get some running done before we adjourned to the shop for the day and I figured she also needed to do her business. So I opened the door and followed her outside and across the yard that was once more beginning to resemble a lawn instead of a muddy morass because the rain, though still an almost daily occurrence, was light and didn't last as long as when it had brought both floods and tornados.

Cleo explored the entire yard, checking out new and interesting smells since her last foray outside the previous evening. Her tail went up, her ears went forward and she headed for the fence around the garden. Something had caught her attention. Another puppy? I hoped not because one Cleo was enough. I waited near the house for her to complete her investigation.

She yipped. Her tail wagged harder. She stared at something unseen and began digging along the garden fence. Whatever she saw was in the garden. I squinted but saw nothing until one of the weeds moved. Something small, brown and furry appeared. A tiny rabbit. A baby small enough to get through a fence designed to keep out both deer and rabbits. It nibbled at the pathetic remains of our garden, going up one side of a row and down the other.

Cleo yipped louder, incensed at being ignored. The tiny rabbit stopped eating and turned towards the puppy. They stared at one another. I didn't know which was more startled, the puppy or the baby rabbit. Or more afraid.

The rabbit made a decision. Cleo was the enemy. It hopped to the corner of the garden, as far from Cleo as it could get as Cleo watched to see what its next move would be. Satisfied Cleo wasn't going to follow it along the fence, it made its move. It slipped through the fence and made a run for the weeds. Cleo went after it.

Cleo would cut it off before reaching the weeds

and the bunny saw that so it made a course correction. It turned and headed my way, running over my feet as it sought to elude Cleo in any way possible. It ended up zipping past Royce's house and across the alley and then past the workshop and into the town of Southfork itself. Cleo, finally registering what the bunny was doing, went after it at top speed.

I didn't know what Cleo's intentions were but wasn't about to let her destroy a tiny, innocent baby rabbit so I yelled for her to stop. She ignored me and speeded up in her pursuit of the bunny. I failed to grab her as she passed me so I followed, running as fast as possible to save one baby bunny from whatever Cleo had planned.

I chased them both around the workshop and past Lottie's store. I was so intent on stopping whatever was about to happen that I failed to look where I was going or whether anyone was in my way.

So it was easy for the men in black hoodies waiting on the sidewalk beside a black car with tinted windows to get me. All they had to do was wait as I plowed into them. Once I'd done so, they stopped my charge with such force that I was lifted off the ground for moments as they grabbed me.

I instantly knew what was happening. Who was holding me. And why. Expressionless faces, bodies with more muscles than I had, and tough, hustled me towards that black car as one of them opened the door so they could throw me inside.

Shock kept me silent for precious seconds. Before they could get me close enough to toss me inside, though, I regained my mind and screamed. Then I screamed again. And again. And again. And I fought like a tiger against the arms holding me.

Royce was still in his house. But he heard.

He ran towards the sound. But Lottie had also heard and grabbed the gun on a shelf behind her counter. She also ran towards my screams. As did George and Lyle, erupting from their stores, who also had pistols handy because Southfork was a tiny hamlet without a police force and they weren't about to become victims should anyone decide to rob them.

Four residents of Southfork armed with guns who knew how to shoot were on their way. The thugs hesitated. They looked around. Lottie, George and Lyle were closing in from one direction and Royce from the opposite direction. We were boxed in.

But the thugs had orders to kidnap me. So they forced me towards the open door of the black car with me fighting each inch of the way.

George's pickup was in front of the feed store to be handy for deliveries. He slid to a stop and jumped in. It flew across the space between the feed store and the black car where he slammed on the brakes and cut the engine. The black car was blocked. There was no way it could go anywhere. It was trapped. The kidnappers were stuck.

They dropped me like a wet rag and looked around for a way to escape the four guns that were heading their way. They ran towards the only opening that would get them away from the stores and the people with guns. They ran flat out towards the stone bridge over the creek.

Royce and the others followed. Royce fired a shot at the running men but he missed. Lottie, George and Lyle picked up speed and barreled towards them. With armed people closing in from two sides, they had no choice. They could either surrender or chance the roiling, muddy water that was just beginning to subside from the dangerous torrent it had been lately.

They jumped. We reached the stone bridge in time to see them struggle with the raging current. I was there also to be as close to the safety of my neighbors and their weapons as possible. If that meant climbing onto the stone bridge with them and watching my captors try to stay afloat in a creek that was doing its best to drown them then I was happy to do so.

Lyle spoke first. "Should we rescue them or let them drown?" They were being swept downstream along with everything the flood had gathered upstream. Logs. Branches. Miscellaneous pieces of furniture. They grabbed whatever was closest that would keep them from going under. "We'll have to go downstream, of course, and grab them as they round a curve and get hung up somewhere."

George had a different take on things. "They'll be in the next county before we can get a rescue organized."

Lottie had a better idea. "Maybe we should just call the sheriff downstream and let his men take care of business."

"Sounds good to me." Royce holstered his pistol and the others stuck theirs in various pockets and they all debated what to do about the men in black hoodies that were now heavy with water and dragging them down.

Royce opened his cell phone and soon was talking with someone who promised to pluck the thugs from the raging water. Whoever it was said, "It'll be like catching carp. Not my preferred catch but best to get them out before they pollute the creek."

It happened exactly as predicted. An hour after Royce's call the soaking men, in prison clothes without black hoodies, were in jail one county over waiting for the FBI to question them about the toys their employers used to smuggle drugs.

"They'll cooperate," was the sheriff's guess. "They are practically dead from almost drowning and are facing years in jail so will be more than happy to rat out anyone they can, especially the employers who sent them on a fool's errand."

It was over. And Cleo had been so distracted by my screams and everything that happened afterwards that she forgot about the baby bunny. It safely disappeared in the weeds a bit beyond the feed store.

Chapter 23

So we could get married. At last. My dress was everything I'd hoped it would be, a frothy creation of tulle and lace that had Royce's eyes growing large as my father escorted me down the aisle in that white church with a classic steeple nestled in a grove of trees just outside of town.

It was a small wedding because it was a small church in a small town. Okay, too small to be a town, Southfork was more like a village. Or a hamlet. Maybe it was a crossroads.

During the reception beneath a canopy on the lawn next to the church, I overheard my father trying to explain what made a place a town instead of a hamlet to my mother who'd probably never been in a small town in her life beyond visits to her in-laws. My grandparents listened to my father's garbled attempts at an explanation and tried not to laugh too hard. "He never was a small town boy," was all my grandfather said. "But I did teach him how to fish so he's not a complete disaster."

My father fished? That was the first I knew about that particular aspect of the man who'd raised me. I tucked the information in the back of my mind for when he and my mother visited. Of course they would visit, even though we lived in a tiny dot on the map, because we were family and they'd want to keep abreast of my life.

I decided to buy a couple extra fishing poles. And waders so my father wouldn't be forced to fish from shore. Then when they came to Southfork for their first visit I'd haul the rods out and smilingly insist he choose one. Then we'd head for the south branch of the Southfork creek and see what he could do.

It would be wonderful. And fun. I'd fish a spot between my father and my husband and we'd all three send our lines through the air in the poetry that was fly fishing. When we were done for the day we'd call my mother over and all of us would watch the sun set over the fields and groves and gently flowing creek of the place that would be my home forever.

Then we'd adjourn to the house Royce and I shared that had enough rooms for a very large family plus all their relations with enough space left over for visitors.

As we'd planned our wedding we'd also agreed on our plans for that house. We'd make full use of it as intended. We'd fill it with our children. After all, it was a family kind of house in a family kind of town – or hamlet – or crossroads – or whatever it was -- and goodness knows Southfork could use a few more people.

THE END

Hi,

I hope you enjoyed *Keeping Susanna Safe*. If you'd like to leave a review, click on the link beneath the *Keeping Susanna Safe* cover on my author's website -- http://www.FlorenceWitkop.com -- and you'll be directed to the Amazon page where you can let people know what you think. Though it's not essential for sales I enjoy hearing from my readers and seeing my books through their eyes.

If you want to see what other books I've written, again, just check out my website – and again, here's the link: http://www.FlorenceWitkop.com

My next book is Soul Wars: *Lexi*. It's a contemporary, clean and wholesome romance with a Christian slant because the bad guy is a demon straight from Hell.

For several years I've been contemplating a romance series that would incorporate demons and all that fire-and-brimstone stuff that is definitely Christian that I love because I'm a Christian who loves scary things that go bump in the night. But I also made sure the *Soul Wars* series will appeal to anyone of any religion – or none – because it can be enjoyed as simply a good action and adventure romance.

There will be more books in the series, though I can't say how often they will be published. Now and then is the only schedule I can promise.

Here's the back cover info that tells what *Soul Wars: Lexi,* is about:

Life was good. Then the whispers began.

Lexi's small business in the laid-back lakeshore town she moved to is promising and the ripped ex-soldier, Zack, who's renovating the house next door is falling for her as hard as she's already fallen for him.

That's on the outside. On the inside she's dying. A demon from Hell whispers in the night and boasts of its plan to steal her life force and her very soul. Unless Zack can save her.

In the military Zack had a well-earned reputation. He's unbeatable. But normal warfighting techniques won't defeat Hell's demons so, with help from some very special townspeople, he sets out to learn new skills and ready himself for the coming battle.

But when the demon comes for Lexi, ready or not Zack must vanquish it utterly or he and Lexi will spend eternity in Hell instead of in that lovely, lakeshore home he's building for them one board at a time.

Can he do it?

Now that you know a little about *Soul Wars: Lexi,* you might enjoy reading the beginning here. It's published by Winged Publications, is available on Amazon, and is free with Kindle Unlimited.

So, until next time,

Florence Witkop

SOUL WARS: LEXI

by

Florence Witkop

CHAPTER 1

I reached the cottage with a sigh of happiness and relief. After two days of driving a tiny, uncomfortable car better suited for city commutes than long distances, I'd reached the cottage with enough daylight left to unload a few things and make dinner before collapsing for an entire night of wonderful, amazing, dreamless sleep. I might sleep until noon.

I got out of my car and meandered across the yard to look for the key my aunt sneakily hid in a hollow in a stump that was all that was left of a tree that had died years before she'd bought the place. A haughty, ceramic gnome sat on top of the stump.

Now, as I crossed the yard, I stopped. Stared in dismay. And gulped. Because instead of sitting on the stump the gnome was scattered about the yard in a thousand pieces. The stump itself was a twisted disaster of rotten wood spread across the front yard in the form of splinters and shards.

Winter storms had obviously been disastrous for both trees and gnomes.

So where was the key? The windows were locked. Probably double locked with deadbolts, thanks to Aunt Gertrude. "No one is getting in my cottage while I'm away. No robbers. No kids looking for a place to party because everything is double locked with deadbolts."

I searched the yard where the stump used to be, hoping to find the key. No such luck. Then, with a look at the sun that was closing towards the horizon while remembering there was no motel in town, I decided desperate situations called for desperate solutions. I'd break into my aunt's cottage.

I could smash a window and replace the glass later. Easy enough. But there was a problem. Though it was a single story building the windows were too high to reach without standing on something. But what?

The only possibilities were my suitcases. So I grabbed the largest suitcase from the trunk of my car and dragged it to the nearest window. It wasn't enough, I needed more height, a familiar problem for five foot something me. So I dragged a second suitcase to the window and piled it on top of the first one.

Still not high enough. The third and last suitcase, though, would do the job, so all I needed was something to break the window with. Since my new business that I'd be starting soon would involve turning junk into treasures, there was a lot of just that in the car. In mere moments I hefted a heavy metal lamp that needed a shade I'd make for it. A gorgeous shade. It was perfect so, lamp in hand, I examined the suitcase pile and reluctantly decided the only way to the top was by climbing and hoping the whole pile stayed in place.

It probably would.

Unfortunately, it didn't.

At the worst possible moment, the suitcase pile moved. Tilted. Slid. With me on it. I screamed. Flailed about. Dropped the lamp. And fell.

I never hit the ground because a pair of very strong arms appeared suddenly from behind and caught me. As the suitcases tumbled every which way I lay in those arms and was glad to be alive and very, very safe.

Until I remembered my manners. I twisted enough to recognize that my savior was a man – though there'd been no doubt about that because those arms were a tribute to muscular male perfection – and said, "Thank you."

The man grunted and turned me to face him. "Who are you and why are you trying to break into a cottage?" Ice blue eyes raked my face and then the rest of me as he said, "You're a thief but you won't rob this place. I'm calling the cops."

I struggled against the arms that held me fast. "I'm not a thief."

"You certainly are." The arms didn't let up, not one tiny bit, as those eyes turned into Antarctic ice. Really cold.

But I managed to talk. Barely. "My aunt owns this cottage but I can't get inside because the key isn't in the stump." I pointed to what was left of the stump. "Because the stump is toast."

Those ice blue eyes narrowed dangerously. "That's not even close to a believable story."

I sagged in those stalwart arms and tried to think how to convince him I was telling the truth. Then I remembered. "My cell phone." I pointed to the car with my phone on the seat. "There are pictures of the cottage on the phone. And more pictures showing where to find the key. And more of me and my aunt. And I can call her. She'll verify my story."

Those eyes lost some of their ice as their owner pondered my words and those unusually strong arms loosened just a bit as I examined the man who'd rescued me but still might send me to jail

He was the most perfect male I'd ever seen.

Slightly over six feet with blue eyes that would surely resemble a summer sky when he wasn't angry, a body that screamed athlete and dark hair cut military short. A soldier or recent veteran?

I soon was showing him pictures of the cottage and more of my aunt and me with the cottage in the background and a couple of the tree stump intact with the gnome on top and last of all, of a tiny, almost invisible hole beneath the gnome's left foot with a key in it.

"See the key? I'm telling the truth."

He folded his arms across his chest, stretching a tee shirt taut that matched tattered shorts that fit just as snugly as the shirt. But he wore excellent and rather expensive running shoes. So he was out for an evening run and had seen what he thought was a break-in.

"Call your aunt." Arms still folded, eyes still with remnants of ice, though not as much as earlier. "Maybe then I'll believe you."

My aunt was on speed dial and answered, her voice sleepy and disoriented from the time difference until she saw the picture I'd taken of the destroyed stump and explained the situation. Then she took a deep breath. "There isn't another key." Followed by, "You'll have to break in."

The man beside me coughed. "Okay. I believe you." And then he smiled and just like that, the entire day glowed as if the sun had suddenly grown a thousand times brighter than when he'd frowned.

Aunt Gertrude had heard him. "Who else is there? Who are you? Can you help?"

The smile grew and there was a hint of an apology in it. "Maybe." He tipped his head and inspected me and I saw him decide to turn that apology into actual help. "Okay, I'll do it. I'll make sure she gets safely inside."

Aunt Gertrude thanked him effusively and went back to sleep and the hunk beside me looked at the metal lamp lying on the ground nearby. "It'll work." He grabbed it and stepped to the window where, without needing suitcases to stand on, he broke the window. Then he continued until all the glass was gone and I could climb safely through.

"Need a lift?" Before I could answer, those arms were around me once more and lifting me and I soon was inside and moments later I had the door open.

"I don't know what I'd have done without you." I hoped he'd answer with something that I could then turn into an invitation for coffee so I could talk to him longer. Get to know him. Salivate a bit. And, most of all, feel good about life in general because I was where I wanted to be and now knew someone local who was also helpful. And nice.

Didn't happen. He shrugged and without another word jogged out to the road and continued with his evening run, leaving me to stare after him and wonder who he was and whether he was married or otherwise taken and a thousand other things I didn't know any more than I knew his name. And he didn't know mine. Or care. Obviously because he'd left without a word.

So I sighed and went inside and found some cardboard and covered the broken window and ate a can of cold spaghetti because after all that had happened, I was too tired to cook. Then I considered sleeping arrangements.

There was one bedroom and a sleeping alcove. I wanted the alcove for an office so I dragged a suitcase into the bedroom. Just one suitcase. The rest could wait, no matter that everything was outside on the grass or in the car. I was that tired.

The bedroom was on the east side of the cottage so the sun would wake me in the morning. I smiled at the thought. Then I climbed into bed and dropped off to sleep expecting to sleep deeply all night long.

Didn't happen.

Around two in the morning by the old fashioned luminous clock on the wall, late enough that I'd got enough rest to be in the lighter phases of sleep, I came suddenly awake. I sat up and stared into the dark and asked myself what had awakened me.

A sound. I'd heard something, I was sure of it.

What kind of sound? I listened for it again. And heard a whisper.

"Lexi."

My name. Who knew I was there? I'd not told anyone where I'd be, not yet. Still, someone knew my name and that I was there. And that someone was in the cottage with me. Unannounced. Uninvited. Unwanted.

It came again. "Lexi Tremaine."

"Who's there?" I spoke bravely into the night but I didn't feel brave. Instead I felt the first faint tremors of fear because I was alone, the nearest town was miles away and the other cottages scattered along the lakeshore weren't occupied yet. Too early in the season.

Whoever was whispering my name had somehow got past the locks I was sure I'd clicked into place. All those deadbolts that kept the cottage secure against winter while it was empty. But there was the window with cardboard on it. Yes, that must be how someone had gotten inside. And they knew my name.

I pulled the blankets to my neck because it made me feel better and called out to the intruder. "What are you doing in my aunt's house?" I tried to sound angry and authoritative. I only succeeded in sounding like a terrified child.

"It's been so long." The whisper became a long-drawn-out sigh. "Soooo long. I'm so tired of waiting."

I held my breath and tried to pinpoint the source of the whisper. In the room, perhaps, because it sounded close, but I could see nothing in the inky blackness as it whispered again. "Lexi Tremaine. At last."

Laughter followed, low and whispery and prolonged and evil. Definitely evil. "I stopped by to introduce myself but I'll let you go back to sleep. This time. And sweet dreams, Lexi." Followed by more whispery laughter that echoed from one wall to another and set my teeth on edge. "You have a while yet. A little while to live and breathe. Then you'll be mine." The whisper finished with, "So, until next time, have a good night Lexiiii. Lexiii. Lexiii." Then it was gone.

Sudden, stunning silence reigned and I somehow knew there'd be no more whispers because whomever was intruding in my life was gone. They'd succeeded in what they were clearly trying to do. To scare me. I was terrified and, though I was sure they were done whispering, they might still be in the cottage.

I forced myself to switch on the bedside lamp. The room was empty but that didn't mean the whisperer wasn't still nearby. He – and it was a male voice, no doubt about that – could be in the kitchen or the alcove or anywhere at all.

I eyed the suitcase on the chair where I'd left it, being too tired to put anything in drawers. There was a twenty-two pistol in that suitcase mere yards away, one I'd bought for protection and taken classes to learn how to use it.

That time had come.

I rose, padded to the suitcase, pulled out the pistol and loaded it as I'd been taught. In a burst of unusual bravery on my part I told myself that whomever was in my aunt's house would be sorry they came.

I approached the door to the rest of the cottage carefully, holding my weapon with two hands, also as I'd been taught, in order to better aim and fire quickly and accurately if someone was on the other side with the intent to do harm. And the voice had made it abundantly clear that was the plan.

But when I kicked the door open no one was on the other side. Nor in the alcove. Nor the main room that made up most of the cottage. Soon the entire building was ablaze with light as I checked every corner of every room, turning on lights and leaving them on as I searched for the whisperer.

He wasn't there.

So where'd he come from and how'd he leave so quickly? I decided to check the locks on the doors. What I found made me suck in my breath and wonder what could be happening because the deadbolts were still in place and there was no evidence of tampering. I checked the windows next. They, too, were closed and securely locked as they'd been all winter with a layer of dust saying they'd not been disturbed. So who had been in the cottage? Even the window that had been broken was still covered with cardboard and tight against the night. How had they entered and how had they left?

Or had the whole thing been my imagination? Could it have been a nightmare?

I put the twenty-two on the kitchen table and made coffee, strong and black because I'd not sleep any more that night so I might as well have something to drink as I waited for dawn and sanity. I sank onto a straight-backed kitchen chair and tried to rationalize what had happened.

Maybe my subconscious was telling me I shouldn't

be trying to start my own business turning discarded things into objects of value. Perhaps I should have stayed in the city instead of coming to this cottage a few miles from a small town along the shore of the lake I'd loved as a child. Maybe it was all too much and an imaginary whisper in the night was the result.

I debated. Could it be the stress of creating a new business? Or of breaking into my aunt's cottage? Or being taken for a burglar? Maybe. As I stared at the twenty-two pistol on the table I came up with lots of reasons why it could have been a nightmare.

The thing was, I was pretty sure none of those things would cause nightmares. Not the business because I didn't need the money, my online marketing business bringing in enough to keep my going until income from the new business kicked in.

And Aunt Gertrude had generously offered her cottage for free while she was in Europe. She said she'd have to pay utilities whether anyone was there or not so if I didn't go overboard on electric usage I didn't even need to worry about that.

And I had no enemies. So what had just happened? I didn't have a clue.

CHAPTER 2

I spent the rest of the night at the table in the brightly lit kitchen as if it was an island of safety in a sea of danger, ignoring that I needed sleep after days of travel. I would take a nap the next day when it was light out and an intruder would be easy to spot if he tried to enter the cottage. If it had been an intruder and not just a bad dream.

I spent those hours staring out the window towards the east and waiting for the sun to rise. I willed it to appear soon and be bright and cheerful. I needed its light to chase away what had surely been the worst experience of my life.

I dug into the bags of groceries I'd bought in the last town and found a chocolate cake and ate a good half of it while waiting for dawn while trying to convince myself that it must, indeed, have been stress even though that made no more sense than any other explanation.

But when dawn finally came and the sun rose high enough for the entire world to be light and the day birds to come out, I followed through on a plan I'd made while sitting at that kitchen table in the middle of the night. I'd find out once and for all if the whisperer was real.

I went outside and circled the entire cottage looking for something – anything – that could send sounds into my bedroom without someone breaking the locks and actually entering the cottage. I looked for a speaker. A megaphone. An electric cord that might have been left by whomever had been there and plugged one end into a recording device and the other into a car battery.

I found no device. Then I looked for footprints or car treads though it hadn't rained so the ground was hard and I feared they might not show. But I examined every inch of my aunt's yard carefully and there surely would have seen something if someone had been there.

Nor did I see car tracks in the driveway other than mine from when I arrived. Since my car had made slight tracks it only made sense that if another car had been there too, there would be additional tire tracks. But there were none.

I decided to make doubly sure, to know without question whether someone was playing a sick joke or not. The whispers were so frightening I needed additional assurance. So I looked past the cottage on its postage stamp sized lakeshore lot.

Could the sound have come from one of the several other cottages scattered along the lakeshore? I decided to check them out, grabbing a sweater against the coolness of the morning and driving slowly along the gravel road that followed the lakeshore with evenly spaced driveways leading to those neighboring cottages, some hidden by trees or undergrowth while others were easily seen perched next to the lake.

I stopped at each and every driveway and looked for evidence of human habitation. I found none. Several of the driveways were behind locked gates that looked like they'd been locked for months judging by the leaves and small branches that would have to be cleared before anyone could drive to the cottages they guarded.

I passed the gorgeous man who'd helped me break into my aunt's house. The man without a name. He was out for another run, in the morning this time, and I examined every inch of his muscular body with awe as we nodded briefly to each other. That was the extent of our encounter though I found myself irrationally wanting to stop him and ask for more help, of the detective kind. He was definitely competent and competence would be appreciated. But I didn't because he'd laugh and those blue eyes would ice up again and I'd freeze to death.

All of the cottages hugged the lake on the way to the tiny town where I'd gotten groceries the evening before. The chocolate cake. But on the other side of my aunt's cottage was a house. A real house, not a cottage, with two stories, a large garage, a shed, and an actual porch overlooking the lake instead of the more usual deck. But I didn't check it out because it was empty and falling down. It wasn't suitable for human habitation. No one could possibly live there.

It had been for sale forever and would probably never sell because making it livable would be a monumental task, never mind that the property was lovely, encompassing acres of woods as well as lakeshore with a swimming beach my aunt had always envied.

After returning from my examination of the cottages between my aunt's cottage and the nearby town, I paused and looked at the trees and tall bushes between my aunt's cottage and that falling-down house. The stretch of wilderness separating the house from my cottage was thicker and wilder than ever and visiting it would require a long walk and I was tired so I decided to check it out some other time.

Then I turned away from the thick underbrush and examined my aunt's cottage – mine for the summer, I reminded myself, and I should start thinking of it that way – and told myself that I'd done enough sleuthing to make sure the whisperer wasn't real. Just a very realistic nightmare.

I entered the cottage and went through to the deck overlooking the lake, determined to enjoy the day and forget the horror of the previous night. I removed the protective cover from one of the two lounge chairs on the deck, stuffed it into the storage bin that held everything anyone could want while outside enjoying the day, and dropped onto the lounge and stared at the lake, lazy blue and almost summer warm.

I lay back and tried to doze but couldn't. My original doubts crept back in spite of knowing the whole thing had been a nightmare. The sun rose high in the sky and then still higher until it brought enough warmth that I discarded my sweater, thinking summer was coming fast and I should stop obsessing over things that hadn't happened and get myself in gear and get my new enterprise going or I'd never have the business I wanted.

I had things to do. Business things. I hadn't even unloaded the car. So I tore my eyes from the riffles over the lake that turned the water into glittering diamonds and ordered myself to get busy.

I didn't get busy. I didn't unload the car. Instead I fell half asleep while looking at the lake, lulled by the warming breeze. The birds trilled in the slice of forest between the cottage and the decrepit house next door until the birdsong put me into a relaxed mood and that was when I realized how stressed I'd been. But no more. I love listening to birds.

I dozed fitfully for an hour or so and finally sat up because the birds refused to let me fall completely asleep. But I wasn't up to unloading the car. So I simply spent the rest of the day in that lounge chair doing nothing except being glad I was there and had finally reconciled reality with nightmares and knew the whisperer wasn't real..

When evening came I was truly exhausted. Several nights with little to no sleep did that. I staggered into the cabin, forgot about dinner and practically fell onto bed. I was too tired to open the windows. I kicked my shoes off, punched the pillow into a semblance of comfort, pulled a blanket over me and fell into the kind of sleep I'd expected to experience the night before.

Didn't happen. As the previous night, I was awakened by a sound. A whisper. Again.

"Lexi."

I didn't sit up this time. Not for a mere nightmare.

Instead I crawled deeper beneath the blankets and pulled the pillow over my head. It didn't work.

"Lexi Tremaine."

I shoved the pillow aside and looked around. I tried to wrap my mind around what was happening. A nightmare that couldn't possibly be a nightmare but neither could it be real. I sat up. "Who are you?" I spoke loudly. Bravely.

The whispery voice laughed indulgently. "Dear, dear Lexi Tremaine. You are so delightful. I enjoy you now and will enjoy you more once you are mine." The voice laughed again with a sinister undertone I'd not noticed before. I hadn't notice it exactly. It had been evil but I'd ignored that aspect of the whispers. Now I couldn't. "And you *will* be mine. No doubt about it." The voice faded but as it did it repeated my name over and over again. "Lexi … Lexi … Lexiiii …" drawing out my name until finally silence reigned.

I spent the rest of that night sitting up and wrapped in blankets because I was afraid to fall asleep. I watched as dawn crept along the shore and reached the cottage and brought a semblance of peace. I should get up and get going and forget about scary nights. But I was also exhausted and needed sleep. The two warred in my mind.

Then, as the sun came fully awake, I heard a sound. Not the whisper of the night. A different sound. A totally different and very real voice. It was loud and boisterous and clearly male and was singing a song that was mostly off tune and was totally, completely, riotously cheerful and happy.

I needed happiness and that song gave it to me. It went straight to my very core. It gave me happiness on a silver platter of joy.

Who was singing? The nearby cottages were empty and I doubted anyone had moved in while I was sleeping. So who was it? And where did the singing come from?

I padded to the sliding door that opened onto the lakeside deck and stepped out to hear better and realized that the house next door, the one on the other side of that green jungle of trees and brush, the one that was a falling down wreck, must be occupied after all because there was no doubt that was where the sound originated.

My first thought was that I wasn't alone and that thought made me realize how frightened the whisper in the night had made me. Now I knew I had a neighbor and he sounded like a nice guy. Moreover, he loved life and the glorious day that was beginning as the sun rose so bright and he also loved music and singing.

I found myself smiling and impulsively started towards the happy sound. Then I stopped because I wasn't ready to meet him. Not yet. What if he was someone I'd want to impress and surely I would want to do just that if for no reason other than to become such good friends that we'd do all sorts of things together and my nightmares would end.

At the moment, though, I should clean up before meeting anyone. My hair was a mess and my clothes were wrinkled from being stuffed in suitcases. I'd wait until I was presentable before making the trek around the forest between our places and introducing myself.

In the bathroom I looked at myself in the mirror in case I was okay for meeting someone. Nope. My hair was a mess and my lack of sleep showed. My eyes were shadowed. My hair was long, to my waist because long hair was uncomplicated and easy to maintain. Few haircuts.

But every inch of that hair now looked pretty much like the jungle between the house and my aunt's cottage and it would take a long time to untangle it, not to mention that it hadn't been washed since before leaving home and was an ugly, dirty brown instead of just brown. And of course, if I hadn't washed my hair, neither had I washed the rest of me. In short, I was a mess. No visit today.

CHAPTER 3

Tomorrow, I decided. I'd meet my new neighbor the very next day. But as I scrubbed my face in a futile attempt to scrub away shadows and washed my hair and the rest of me and combed that hair into a semblance of normalcy and finally toweled off, clean and dry, I was glad to have heard that raucous song.

With every window open to hear better, I listened to the singer's next song and the one after that and then still more as morning and then afternoon wore on. I wondered what my neighbor was like and what the house that had been falling down for so many years would be like and decided it would be beautiful because the person living there now would have turned it into a place of happiness and beauty. Of course he did, he loved music and so would insist on a beautiful home.

I didn't get a single thing done that day because all I did was listen to those off-key songs that healed my fear and raised my spirits and made me happy.

A lot must have been accomplished with that house in the past year. Construction crews. Builders. Painters. Gardeners. And more. I found myself looking forward to whatever transformation had taken place and to getting to know the owner.

I went to bed that night thinking about the house next door and the unknown man who lived there. The singer.

I went to bed. But I didn't sleep. Of course I didn't. Because the whisperer returned.

As I heard the now familiar hissing come through the night, I surprised myself by knowing in some deep place in me I'd not known existed until that moment that wherever the whispers originated wasn't the real world.

That knowledge – and it was an awareness as much

as real knowledge -- had been building in my subconscious since that first night and somehow, for some unknown reason, that night the knowing solidified. Where it came from I couldn't know. But I knew it to be true.

I tried to ignore the whispers. Perhaps I partially succeeded because they didn't last as long as the other nights and when they finally ended I managed to get enough sleep to actually get some rest. Not much, but some.

The next morning I took a long shower and rinsed my face with cold water to wake me up until, staring into the bathroom mirror I decided I looked better than the day before. It was time to meet my neighbor.

There were n o raucous, happy songs, not yet, but it was early and just knowing someone was nearby made me feel better. He didn't have to sing all the time, just often enough for me to know I wasn't alone and for me to steal some of the happiness those songs scattered about so freely.

I grabbed a quick breakfast, pulled a brush through my too-long hair and managed to untangle it for the third time that morning, checked myself for the hundredth time in the mirror and then I went out the sliding glass doors to the deck overlooking the lake and from there to the beach, slogging through the sand barefoot even though it was cold. I walked past the thick forest between my aunt's cottage and the house next door. Looked to see what had been done to the disaster of a place.

And stopped in stunned surprise.

Not because it was suddenly transformed into a showplace. It wasn't. It was pretty much as I remembered from past years except the worst of the mess had been torn away and was now in a dumpster beside a tent erected in the yard with a very large table in front of it.

There were things in the yard that spoke of construction. A pile of fresh, new-smelling lumber. Boxes of what I guessed to be hardware of various types though it was hard to tell because they were covered against the weather by tarps that were staked to the ground. Roof shingles, light gray in color, were far enough to one side that they most likely weren't to be used soon. And so on.

Clearly the construction was barely begun and the singing I'd heard was by one of the construction workers instead of the owner, though what purpose the tent served I couldn't imagine. An office, perhaps, because of the table in front, though what office would have a desk outside where office equipment could get wet whenever it rained? And there wasn't any business equipment on the table.

I took a few steps closer to see what was on it and was rewarded by the sight of a coffee mug and a thermos jug, plus a plastic box containing donuts. Yep, it belonged to the construction crew.

I was curious to see more of the remodel while

knowing it was wrong to trespass. But curiosity got the better of me and I went to the house anyway to see what was being done. I stepped through the doorway that no longer had a door and into the interior of a house that had been gutted to its bare bones. Only the exterior walls and the floors remained intact and in some places even those were open to the weather. I could see lapping waves on the beach through window frames that no longer had windows in them, being mere rectangular spaces in the walls.

I looked closer. Some of the walls – the ones facing the lake – had chalk lines drawn on them. I tipped my head in thought until it came to me what they represented. Places where large windows would be placed that would give a gorgeous view of my favorite lake. I liked whomever had insisted on those views without having met him. Or her. Or them. The new owners whomever they were.

As I considered the chalk lines designating where new, huge windows would go I realized that several were placed for perfect viewing of the wilderness just outside the house. Which could be why it was still wild. Because they wanted it pristine so they could watch wildlife up close.

Having seen what I could, I returned to the beach and then headed back to my aunt's cottage, toes once more digging deep in the cold sand.

If the new owners weren't happy people, I decided, it didn't truly matter because the remodel would surely take at least the entire summer, if not longer, so for the entire time I'd be living in the cottage I'd have the company of the cheerful construction crew and those happy, cheerful, off-key songs.

Which meant it would be a good summer. I danced in the sand as I made my way back to my cottage. Tried to dance though I was more bogged down than light footed because I just knew the sounds of happy songs would chase away the whispers in the night starting tonight.

I'd introduce myself to the construction crew as soon as possible and let them know I liked music. Maybe I'd bring donuts.

Then I heard a sound. It came from the thicket between the cottage and the house under construction. I stopped, unsure whether to run as fast as possible or stand my ground to intimidate what must surely be some large, dangerous animal. The trees and bushes were large enough to hide anything.

I raised my arms as people were told to do when confronted with a large, dangerous animal because it would make me look larger than I am and more dangerous. I huffed and puffed and waited to see what would emerge from what I now considered a dangerous though rather small forest.

A woof came to me as a puppy, black and white and cute, meandered out of the trees and came to me. It rubbed itself against my ankles and I deflated. My attacker wasn't dangerous after all. He was cute and friendly and wanted to be picked up and was a 'he,' that was obvious after a quick peek at his underside.

Where did he come from? The obvious answer was the house under construction because he surely didn't belong to any of the empty cottages along the lakeshore. One of the workers had a puppy.

"What's your name?" I asked and he answered by rubbing against my legs still more, asking for love and attention. "I'd love a four-legged visitor every so often and I'm here for the summer."

The puppy responded by following me to my cottage and into the main room where I found some leftover food that would work for treats and he knew exactly what I was doing which meant he was used to being pampered.

"Now what?" I went onto the deck and he followed. I sank into one of the lounge chairs and he climbed onto my lap and looked at me with the sure expectation of tummy rubs and more love, which I gave because my life lately had been horrible and puppy love reminded me it was good.

I pampered him for a long time. But eventually I had to get some work done so I dumped him off my lap and headed for my car to finally – finally – unload it and get started on that new business I was hoping would become profitable enough for me to make a living and I'd better get started or it would never earn a dime.

The puppy followed and then followed still more as I made trips back and forth between the car and the cottage and kept me company for a while. But as it became evident I was going to work instead of pampering him any longer he bid me farewell and disappeared around the forest between my cottage and the house under construction.

I finished emptying my car, load after load until the car was bare and the cottage was full of boxes and bags and miscellaneous things strewn about because some of the things I'd brought just didn't fit into neat containers. And looked like trash. Because it was trash.

It was the stuff I'd got by dumpster diving for things I could repurpose into useful and/or beautiful things that I could sell in person and online for enough money to support myself.

CHAPTER 4

I spent the rest of that day stowing things in corners and on tables and behind doors until I could at least walk through the cottage without tripping over some piece of junk that would become something beautiful once I'd figured out what it would become and had actually done the repurposing.

I broke for lunch but went back to work immediately after cleaning up after myself. I heard the singing again and smiled, thinking of the singer and the puppy having a good time together but I didn't go around the thicket between our houses because now that I'd finally gotten started I wanted to get my own house in order so I could get my new business going as soon as possible.

After I was done unloading, a trip to the nearby small town was next on my to-do list to do more dumpster diving and see if there were stores where I could sell my finished items.

It was a tourist town, I knew that much, so figured

there'd be stores selling lovely items, both useless and useful, to visitors that would remind them of their special time there. Hopefully, some of those items would be mine.

I sighed in contentment just thinking about the future opening before me. And also because the singing next door was so happy that it made me happy and the thought of possible visits from a cute, friendly black and white puppy made my smile even broader.

I ate dinner on the deck watching the sun set over the water and the stars come out bright and clean. I stayed up late because it was a lovely night even though it was still early enough in the season that I retrieved a blanket from the bedroom and wrapped myself in it to keep warm as I took in the night sights and sounds.

I only went to bed when I started nodding off. I didn't want to sleep on the deck and wake up in the morning with a crick in my neck because I had a full day ahead that involved finding both more junk to turn into beautiful items and a place to sell some of them. That would be in the afternoon, of course, after I met the construction crew in the morning. Especially the singer of happy songs. And the owner of the puppy.

When I couldn't stay awake one second longer I dragged the blanket after me into the bedroom and locked the sliding glass doors securely because the whispers had made me overly conscious of being alone and it just seemed like a reasonable precaution in spite of the fact that I was in a laid-back rural area where crime was unknown and I'd had the glass replaced in the window that has been broken. And the locks changed, of course.

I didn't expect any whispers that night. They no

longer held a spell over me and would never repeat. Puppy love and happy, off-key songs and the smell of new wood had chased them away forever.

About that, I was wrong.

"Lexi."

I came awake, stomach heaving because how could it happen again? "Who are you?" I screamed into the night, past fear, past anything except pure, unadulterated anger. I screamed again. "Leave me alone or I'll call the cops."

Laughter. Whispered laughter. "I so enjoy you, Lexi. Your sense of humor. Your useless threats."

"You're not real!" I screamed louder if such was possible, unsure whether I was glad the windows were shut so my screams wouldn't wake my neighbor or whether I wished they would. "You can't do anything because you're not real!"

More laughter echoed from wall to wall, whispered laughter but it came clearly through the inky black of the night. "Oh, I'm real, Lexi. I'm very ancient and very, very real."

"Leave me alone!" By then I didn't know if I was screaming or sobbing or both. I threw my pillow against the wall, hoping against hope I'd hit something. A shadow. A ghost. Anything, real or not. "I'm not afraid of you."

This time the laughter lasted for almost a minute. "Yes you are afraid of me, Lexi. You're very afraid and you're going to grow more and more afraid over time and that's just what I want."

"I'm not afraid and I'll laugh louder each time you bother me."

"No you won't, Lexi. I know you so I know you

are afraid – terrified – and each time I come your fear will grow until it consumes you. And weakens you."

"It won't!"

The whisper clucked softly. "And when the process is complete – when every cell in your body is afraid and weak and can't fight me any longer – then you will be mine."

I threw the second pillow at the opposite wall and the same thing happened as when I threw the first one. Nothing. Absolutely nothing.

Except fear. Because I knew with a primitive kind of bone-deep knowledge that something evil was behind the whisper. And it wanted me. I knew with that same bone-deep knowledge that if I couldn't figure how to stop it, would have me. I faced the fact that whatever whispered in the night was real and evil and wanted me. And would eventually own me.

I got out of bed, turned on the light, pulled that twenty-two from where I'd decided it belonged, in the bedside table, and flashed it about in a melodramatic but useless gesture.

"Tut tut, Lexi, Bullets can't hurt me. They'll merely put holes in your aunt's walls and you'd have to explain why you shot up her cottage and chances are she'll call the nearest insane asylum and then every chance you might have of defeating me will be gone because such places are where I do my best work."

I put the pistol back in the shallow drawer and slammed it shut as I heard what the whisperer had just said. I had a chance to defeat it. Just a chance. But I'd take it. "I don't need a pistol. I will simply ignore you until you crawl back to wherever you came from like the scum you are."

"Lexiiii, Lexiiii, Lexiiii."

I'd already figured out that when he drew my name out like that and said it slowly it meant he was taking his leave. "See you later, Lexiiii. Sweet Lexiiii. My Lexiiii."

Then the whisper was gone and silence came as swiftly and completely as if it had never happened. I sat up in bed, wide awake, pulled my knees to my chin and waited for dawn and the hope that comes with every new day as I prayed with every fiber of my being for that construction worker to be next door singing because I desperately needed his songs.

The sun came up as it always does and I crawled out of bed and padded to the bathroom. In the mirror I looked somewhat normal. Not completely normal but better than those first days.

Then something wonderful happened. I heard singing. Loud, boisterous, happy and totally offkey. It seemed so close I wondered if the singer was on the deck and had come for a visit, so I turned to look but it was empty. When I turned back to the mirror, however, the shadows were disappearing and I knew they were vanquished by my unknown singer. I smiled at my reflection and thanked whoever sang so badly for giving me the strength to face the day.

I didn't even pull a brush through my tangled mess of hair because I was in that much of a hurry to meet him. I forgot to wear shoes, dashing along the cold early spring sand and not noticing as I ran beside the jungle of trees and bushes that pretty much resembled my hair. A mess.

I stopped before reaching my neighbor's yard. Moved close to the thick forest and hid behind a tree.

And slowly, cautiously, as sneakily as possible, peered around it to inspect the construction crew and identify the singer.

My mouth dropped open in surprise. And shock. Because there was no crew. Instead, there was just one man carrying a dozen or more new two-by-fours from a pile on the edge of the yard towards the house.

One man. Not a crew. But it was the identity of that single man that made me stand without moving. Without thinking With my mouth open.

Because that one lone man was the man who'd rescued me when I fell off a pile of suitcases. My savior who'd gotten me safely in the cottage. Now I knew he was also the man who sang the songs that drifted on the air and reached me and reminded me the world was a good place. Totally off-key songs sung by a man whose smile turned the world bright and could surely – surely – chase an evil whisperer away. If he chose to do so..

He was tall, masculine and competent, self-assured, and gorgeous in a totally male, military, guy's guy kind of way. And he lived next door.

I took a deep breath and stepped from behind the tree and walked towards him to introduce myself and I forgot how to breathe when he noticed me.

He stopped carrying those two-by-fours and dropped them carefully to the ground and we stood there without speaking for the longest time, staring at each other over those two-by-fours in the heat of the day with a black and white puppy running between us.

Then he smiled and, yes, it was that same thousand-watt smile and I knew – just knew – that no whisperer in the night could ever frighten this man and I wondered how I could get him to stay with me the next time I was afraid.

He nodded to me. He remembered me. And came towards me with a ground-eating stride that spoke of male confidence and lots of hard physical work.

www.ingramcontent.com/pod-product-compliance
Lightning Source LLC
Chambersburg PA
CBHW070419310726
48977CB00003B/761